A GOOD LONG WAY

ALSO BY RENÉ SALDAÑA, JR.

The Case of the Pen Gone Missing /
El caso de la pluma perdida

A GOOD LONG WAY

René Saldaña, Jr.

PIÑATA BOOKS
ARTE PÚBLICO PRESS
HOUSTON, TEXAS

A Good Long Way is made possible through grants from the City of Houston through the Houston Arts Alliance.

Piñata Books are full of surprises!

Arte Público Press
University of Houston
452 Cullen Performance Hall
Houston, Texas 77204-2004

Cover design by Mora Des!gn
Photo by Matthew Crawford

Saldaña, Jr., René
  A Good Long Way / by René Saldaña, Jr.
    p. cm.
  Summary: Three Mexican American teenagers in a small-town in Texas struggle with difficulties at home and at school as they try to attain the elusive status of adulthood.
  ISBN 978-1-55885-607-3 (alk. paper)
  [1. Family problems—Fiction. 2. Emotional problems—Fiction. 3. Runaways—Fiction. 4. Schools—Fiction. 5. Brothers—Fiction. 6. Mexican Americans—Fiction. 7. Texas—Fiction.] I. Title.
PZ7.S149Go 2010
[Fic]—dc22

2010032989
CIP

Printed in the United States of America
October 2010–November 2010
Versa Press, Inc., East Peoria, IL
12 11 10 9 8 7 6 5 4 3 2 1

CHAPTER ONE

ROELITO—2:34 AM, March 27TH

I hear the sound of feet shuffling—more like stomping, really—coming from somewhere in or around the house, but I can't tell exactly where from. Anyhow, it's this stomping that startles me awake. I'm pretty groggy. I'd been sleeping for two, maybe three hours now. Earlier, when it was still yesterday, I was cramming for my Algebra I midterm, a monster of a test as a matter of fact. I was worried the whole week leading up to it because I want to keep my A in Mr. Ramírez's class. After studying for several hours before trying to catch some zs, and then an hour or so of lying in bed, all still and quiet, forcing my eyes closed, I was still worried and anxious. No lie, it was sixty minutes worth of turning onto my right side, then the left, flipping onto my stomach, then on my back again, over and over, and then finally I got to sleep.

And now I'm awake, upset because my clock reads 2:34 AM. That's the middle of the morning. The darkest part of morning. I'm fuming mad, practically grinding my teeth. *Who's making this racket?* I wonder. *Who's messing up my chances at a solid grade on my test?* I'd been hoping for a few good hours of sleep, but it's obvious from the noise still going on that those plans are shot. I close my eyes again, put my head under the pillow to muffle the noise and maybe force myself back to

1

sleep, trying to convince myself I only imagined the noise, that heavy shuffling I heard. But there it is again.

So I roll out of bed, huffing now because I won't be getting the proper amount of sleep. I glance over at my brother's bed, but it's still made from yesterday morning. His schoolbooks, that he's taken to carrying old style, tied together with an old leather belt, are on the desk, same place where he left them—what?—two weeks ago. The door's open a few inches, and I remember having shut it. My dad had been up watching some television in the next room, and I closed the door to keep out the light from the TV screen and the newscasters' voices. I needed to study in peace and quiet. Right now, I pull on the door, thinking that maybe if I close it, that'll take care of the noise and I can go back to sleep, but it won't close like it should. I see that at the foot of it, acting like a doorstop, are my brother's shoes, socks, and the shirt he'd worn to school yesterday.

I've made my way through most of the living room now, and I can see the door facing the porch is open. A few feet from the door, I can hear the noise more clearly, louder. It's people whispering, plus the shuffling. But they're not soft whispers, more like a scratching at the back of your throat. I can tell it's my brother, Beto, and my dad, Beto, Sr. I creep closer to the front door, careful not to whack my shins against the side table, and when I'm passed it, I put my back up against the wall. Now I hear them screaming but whispering at the same time. For the past several weeks Dad and Beto have been yelling at each other now and again. Beto's a senior in school, about to graduate, "a man already," he insists, "so why can't you treat me like one, Dad?" And my dad, angry, disappointed because Beto's been coming home after what Dad calls "a very reasonable curfew," and, worse, smelling of smoke and beer, like a *cantina*.

"A real man knows about lines, *m'ijo*," Dad maintains. "And he doesn't cross the important ones."

Tonight's shouting, though, is different from all those other arguments; there's an urgency to this one. Almost like they're each taking off in opposite directions and this is the end of the line for both of them, each leaving the other forever, and they're yelling like they have too much to say before parting ways but not enough time to say it all. So, they're screaming it. As if saying it louder will help say it all. There are levels of meaning in the shouting, too. There's the literal meaning, the words themselves spilling out of their mouths. Then there's the pitch, taut and higher than their regular, everyday talking. And there's the scraping of the consonants at the back of their throats, so scratchy it's got to hurt. And the speed of it all, too. Each means something, and it's all bad.

I look out the front door, and I get scared all of a sudden. I had thought all it was going to be was one stomping away and scream-whispering, then the other following closely after and whisper-shouting, back and forth, causing that shuffling that woke me. At worst, them standing face to face, chests puffed out, my dad's finger smack-dab in Beto's face to make his point clear, Beto staring back hard, taking the finger in his face and letting it go at that, but Beto is yelling right back at Dad, just as ugly. My dad is waving his arms wild in the air, his hair and Beto's just as wild, Beto putting an open palm up to Dad's face, a sort of "Shut up, old man."

From what I'm seeing right now, it's obvious I imagined it all wrong, though. It's worse than anything I could have thought up.

I'm through-and-through awake now. And my math test coming up tomorrow is light years away. It matters little to me right at this moment. My heart's beating so hard it's throbbing, first at my throat, then at my temples. I'm shaking, frightened at what I'm seeing unfold before me. Right at the screen door now, I can just make out my father and Beto in the darkness, behind the blur of the mesh. I'm scared stiff. I notice a rip in the screen door at about shoulder height, and in other places the mesh is bulging inward, where elbows and fists missed their intended marks and tore instead against the screen. I push open the screen door and step out. I'm right on them.

The two of them are twisting and pushing at each other. Beto's got a clump of Dad's shirt in one hand and with the other he's gripping Dad's shoulder. Dad's got his own fist full of crinkled shirt in one hand and the other's clamped down on Beto's elbow. It's almost like they're hugging, but it's not that at all. It's a fight, an honest-to-goodness fight. I can just make out some swelling on their faces. Or am I just imagining that? It would mean they've actually punched at each other, and though Dad did spank us when we were kids, he hasn't laid a hand on either one of us since. I know Beto would never raise a hand to Dad. But then again, I never thought he'd be acting quite like this either.

I shake my head to clear all of this confusion. I can see how serious this is in their eyes, how there's anger in both of their looks, not hatred, but an explosion finally of all the frustration that's built up over the last few weeks. More than a mere skirmish, but something full-blown and well past trying to take back.

I still don't know what's going on. I stand there and stare. I mean, my dad and my brother are going at it hard.

I don't get it. They're father and son, for goodness' sake. How can they be doing this?

I can't stand doing nothing myself, so I jump at them. I wedge myself between them, first an arm, then my whole self. I have to push hard, and even where I'm at they still don't know I'm there. They're looking past me, through me, beyond me. At each other. I don't exist right at that moment. I can smell their anger in the odor coming from their pits, in their hard, bitter breath. They're all sweaty, slippery. Still pushing and pulling, roaring at each other, words I can't understand because they're not meant for me, but for each other's ears only. But the gist of the words is clear as day. The substance of them is in their bared teeth, in the grappling with one another: *¡Ya basta!* is what my dad means to say, and *¡Ya basta!* is what Beto wants to get across. And when enough is enough but no one seems to want to give even an inch, sometimes it comes to blows.

They crinkle their eyes, and finally they begin to take notice of me.

And now the pushing eases.

I'm facing my dad, my back to Beto. I see the shadow of a beard on my father's cheeks, that's how close I am to him. Close enough to see the gold on one of his teeth. To smell garlic on his breath from dinner. Maybe even cilantro. And on my neck, I feel Beto breathing on me. Hot breath, and his chest heaving on my shoulder. They're two bulls snorting. And I'm stuck between them, them blind to me. Eyes only for each other.

So, lost there, invisible between them, I start crying: "Stop it. The two of you, stop it! You're father and son, you should love each other. You . . . you stupids!"

One of them gives a little, then they both give, and in the giving one of them, I don't know which, slaps me on the side of the face. I know he didn't mean to hit me, but he did, and I'm crying now, sniveling like a baby, running at the nose, and that's when they separate. They let go of everything.

So I turn, give them each a trembling shoulder, make a bit of room for myself between them, a bit of room for them too.

"Shake hands," I tell them trembling. When they don't, I say it again in a hard whisper of my own this time: "I said shake."

They finally notice it's me there between them telling them to shake hands, and most likely they don't hear me because they're not shaking like I want. Shaking their heads instead, catching their breath.

I hear a noise coming from inside the house. It's Mom. She's crying, too. She must be in the living room close enough to the door to hear and see what's just happened. But I can't see her when I turn for a brief moment to look for her. *Why isn't she coming out to help me?* I wonder. *And don't Dad and Beto hear what they're doing to her? Do they care more about themselves than for her feelings? What jerks!*

I turn back to the porch when my dad tells Beto, "No more, Beto. You wanna stay in this house—*my* house— there's rules you gotta follow. If you don't wanna respect that, *pues vete.* Get out." He doesn't scream it. The old man just says it, all calm now, which is even scarier to me than when he was whisper-yelling. This means to me that he's dead serious, leaving no room to take a step back.

"*¿Sabes qué?*" Beto says in that same cold-metal voice. He is so our father's son. "I'm out of here then. Laters." He shoves me into my father, leaps off the porch, and cuts down the front yard. There, he turns the corner and is gone before I catch my balance.

I look at my dad, then back at the corner of the house where Beto disappeared, but he can't have gone far yet, so I jump down from the porch and run after him. Behind me Dad slams the screen door shut.

I look into the darkness and scream after my brother: "Beto, Beto! Stop! Please come back, Beto! Let's talk a little. What's going on, man?" I'm still crying. All I see of him now is his back, better said, the shadow of his back. He doesn't turn, doesn't stop. He's getting smaller, reaching the fence at the end of our yard. There's nothing I can do to catch up to him. He's way too fast, way too focused on getting out of here.

It's just a few moments past, but all I see in the black of the backyard is a specter of him, then he does stop, turns. He's gotten as far as the fence. Even at this late hour, I can tell he looks at me, his chest heaving, his arms at his sides, loose as though nothing like what's gone on just now has happened, like he's waiting for a game of basketball to start up. No hint in his body language that he and Dad just had it out.

I say, "Can't we talk? Come back, will you? You and Dad just have to . . . "

He looks down at the ground and shakes his head. "No more talk, little brother. It's way past talk. *Nos vemos.*"

"Where'll you go?" I say. "You've got nowhere to go. Just come back."

"I got a place. Later, bro."

And the next second he's gone, running down the alleyway.

I'm standing still, wondering, *What just went on?*

Alone in the darkness of the backyard, the blinking stars overhead, the cold of the dewy grass on my feet, I feel myself still shaking.

BETO—2:42 AM, March 27TH

Beto said to himself, "Plenty places for me to be besides here." He turned and took the fence in one leap. He ran hard down the alley. It was dirt from one end of the barrio to the other, and Beto headed in the direction of the highway, but he had no idea really where he'd end up. Every few seconds he'd take a quick peek over his shoulder to see if Roelito was following him. Which he wasn't. He ran faster. His feet were burning on the cold, dusty pathway. That's when he noticed he was still bare-foot.

Earlier in the night, before having it out with his dad, Beto had come in way past curfew. His dad had told him midnight and no later. But Beto thought he was old enough to come in when he felt like it, to not be treated like a baby, being told when and when not to do this or that. He'd told his dad this enough times already, so the old man would lay off him, but he hadn't. Got after him every time he caught Beto breaking one of his "rules." And they always argued, which usually ended with Beto getting quiet, real quiet, staring at the floor in front of him and taking whatever Beto, Sr. doled out.

Tonight, after coming in from playing pool with some of the guys, Beto tried to be silent, not because he was scared of his dad, but because he didn't want the hassle. So, he took off his shoes outside on the porch and snuck in, all quiet-like.

Just outside his and Roelito's bedroom, he took off his socks and unbuttoned his shirt. He didn't want to wake the kid up. Beto had seen him studying all week for this math test. The kid took this school business seriously.

Beto thought, *My little brother's solid that way*. He shook his head smiling. His baby brother was a hoot. A real nerd, already talking about graduating either first or second in his class. Sending away for information from several universities across Texas, a few from outside the state. And as soon as a new fat envelope arrived, Roelito would tear through the pamphlets. The kid even took notes. And when Beto asked, "What's that you're writing?" Roelito answered, "Jotting down which place meets the most of my criteria." Beto looked at the notes once and noticed that most, if not all, of the highest ranking were far away from home. He had the right idea in mind: Get out of dodge quick. Roelito was also saving some of his cash to buy SAT study guides.

"You're a López, *ese*," he'd told Roelito once. "It's got to be the best place for you. *¿Me entiendes, Méndez?*"

Roelito had said, "I get what you're saying. Thanks, B." The kid was dedicated. Studied his butt off.

Beto had been tired tonight, so he would finish undressing out here, and then tiptoe in. He was halfway pulling his shirt off when he felt his dad's hand grab hold of him by the shoulder and force him around. He could hear his baby brother snoring just beyond the door behind him—he imagined the math book lying beside Roelito, who'd be sprawled out on the bed, his hand still clutching his mechanical pencil, papers scattered everywhere. Beto heard his dad grinding his teeth, the anger in his breathing.

"*Órale*, what's the deal, *jefe*?" he said. "No need to be like that." That's when they'd stepped outside onto the porch.

"*¿Cómo te atreves, m'ijo,* coming in at this hour?" His dad took a step up to Beto and took a whiff. "And smelling like a *borracho* besides?"

Beto said, "Whatever. I don't drink, like I've told you before," and turned to go back in.

Beto, Sr. forced him around again, crunching Beto's shirt at the neck. "Don't ever turn your back on me."

"You're one to talk, *viejo.*"

That's how it'd been tonight—psh, for the past several weeks, truth be told: pushing pulling pushing pulling. A ton of shouting, too. They'd been going at it hard for a while when Roelito had come out.

And now Beto was running. But he'd left behind his shirt, socks, and shoes. Just outside the bedroom door.

Beto slowed down. He was almost at the end of the dirt alley. He looked over his shoulder again, and when he saw no one was following—not Roelito, not his dad—he stopped and crouched by a light pole, leaned back on it, and caught his breath, filling his lungs with the cool night air. *Man,* he thought. *Why'd the kid have to come out like that? See us acting like animals? See me like that? Shoving our dad like I did?* "Stupid," he said and punched at his thigh. Beto had been angry when his dad grabbed him and pulled him outside. Not thinking anything, just reacting. So he'd been ugly like that with his dad. He wasn't high on dope, or drunk, or hadn't been smoking. Just hanging out at the pool hall, shooting some stick. The guys there smoked, sure. Drank, too, but he didn't. Ever. So he got mad when his dad accused him of it again tonight, and why did the old man have to treat him like he had? All disrespectful like that? *What else could I have done?* he thought. He looked down the alley again. No Roelito, no dad, no one. He was on his own.

He clasped his hands and stretched his arms over his head. Roelito had been right asking him where he was headed, saying he had no place to go. This was it for him. He had run out of alley. Next was to cross the highway, then there were the fields and more fields after them. Then what? He'd never been out that far. To the left, about three, four miles, there was the school, but that was no place to go. To the right, the town of Mission about seven miles, then McAllen about another seven, eight miles. But Beto didn't know those places. They were bigger towns, McAllen almost a city. No way he wanted to get lost in either of those places.

He'd caught a good breath now, and he said, "Think, Beto, think. Where to now?"

He heard dogs barking. There was the quiet of houses full of families settled in for the night. He saw porch lights on outside those houses, part of the barrio ritual: a light on at night to keep away the bad element. He knew his own father would have switched on the front porch light by now.

It came to him. He'd go over to Jessy's house. She'd be awake reading or listening to music. He could hang out with her. He'd have to retrace his steps down the alley, but not all the way back to his own yard. Just up a ways.

When he reached Jessy's house, Beto walked carefully from tree to tree, occasionally looking over his shoulder, or squinting into the darkness ahead. He stopped at the last tree and listened, looked, then quickstepped on his tippy toes to the side of the house. He didn't want to think what Jessy's dad would do to him tonight if he busted Beto outside his house.

His back to the wall, Beto edged his way along it, and at the front corner nearest the trees, he got down on all fours and crawled behind the bougainvillea hedge that lined the front of the house. He was almost at her window. He made his way cautiously, quietly, and slid into the dent he'd worn into the ground under the ledge. He waited. When Jessy's dad didn't come out into the front yard pointing a shotgun every which way, Beto breathed easy. The dirt was cold on his bare feet.

Jessy was his best friend from growing up in the barrio all their lives, and she'd know what Beto's next step should be. She'd run away a couple times before. Beto thought he had it hard at home, but he knew his life was Easy Street compared to hers. Nobody knew this about her. Everybody at school thought she was a hard-core gangster the way she dressed, all baggy with punchy hair. Sure, she was tough, but man, she was also soft. Beto knew that side of her. He'd held her a couple times while she cried it all out of her system after her dad had come home from drinking the whole day and night and beat on her mom.

She was smart besides. Nothing worse than a smart chick with a tough-as-nails attitude, staring those teachers down sometimes, zapping them with electric sparks coming out of her eyes. But she was more soft than anything else, if you were willing to take a more careful look at her. Those teachers just saw a waste of their time in her and just never gave her a shot. They gave up on her. *And they call me a quitter*, Beto thought. None of these principals or teachers ever looked at her. *At* her. At *her*. Her real self, the everyday Jessy, the one under the black T-shirts, the one who listened to classical music on her headset when everybody just knew she had to be listening to some punk metal or goth. If they only knew her like he did, the whole school would be in tears and hugging on each other.

The lights in the house were all off, even Jessy's. But Beto knew she was up, she almost always was, a whole different life under the cover of her blanket. Even if she were asleep, she'd be there for him. He'd woken her a few times before and they'd talked and talked. She'd know where he should go next.

He listened for the fuzzy buzz of the music. Nothing. Then he raised himself onto his knees and peeked in the window. Dark. Except for a dull light under the tent of Jessy's blanket. He scratched at the screen and whispered, "Hey, Jessy. Jessy."

He scratched again, and the light went out. There was silence for the next several seconds. Only the stillness of quiet. He could see the silhouette of the tent, though.

"It's me, Jessy—Beto." He scratched. "Beto, Jessy."

Then he heard rustling, but quiet otherwise. Then no sounds. Beto strained to see what was happening inside, beyond the screen, and almost fell back when she whispered right in his face, "What's up, Beto?"

She'd just appeared like that. He could smell the cinnamon toothpaste on her breath. She was so close he could have kissed her.

"Hey," he said.

"It's 3:04. What you doing still up?"

"Not reading like some people."

"You just coming back from pool?"

"Nah. Been there and back."

He was beginning to make out her face now, a bit fuzzy because of the screen, but definitely there, looking right at him.

"Running away."

With her hair loose and soft like tonight, Beto could fall in love with her. Not best friend sort of love, but *love* love. Like grow old with her and take care of her for the rest of her life kind of love.

"What?"

"Yeah, the old man and me had it out finally. It was a bad scene, and he said he don't want me home no more. So I'm taking off. Got any ideas where to?"

She didn't say.

"Maybe I can sleep on your floor?"

"Yeah, whatever," she said. "Let my dad walk in and catch you, you'd think your run-in with your dad was cake. Never mind what patch of beating I'd catch. You can stay out there till morning if you want. I'll pass you a quilt or something."

"No way. Ground's too hard, and cold."

"Beggars can't be choosers, baby."

"Yeah. But still . . . You still got my bag?"

"Yup," she said. "Wait here."

JESSY—3:12 AM, March 27TH

You get up from kneeling next to the windowsill and walk quietly into the darkness of your room. Beto seems nervous to you. All jittery. Same look as your mom's earlier tonight. Both of them, at wit's end. Lost.

For the past two weeks or so, Beto'd been telling you he was going through with this any day now, but he'd been saying so for years now, too. At the window you thought you made out some dark blotches on his right cheekbone, cry-bags under his eyes, so tonight was his night, for real. He'd gone and done it—was cold, alone, and scared.

You know the feeling. You'd taken off a few times yourself. So you know what place he's at right now. Probably staring into your bedroom trying to make out your shadow, not wanting to lose sight of you, thinking you're his last hope, sad you didn't let him come in, offering instead the cold ground outside. Not inside, though. Not with your dad in his bad way and just a few feet down the hallway.

As cold as it is, you know letting Beto in would be the biggest mistake, sure. Your dad never checks in on you this late, but better safe than sorry. Real sorry if he just out of the blue happened to look in and found a boy in your room. Sorry him, sorry you.

You pull the closet door open as softly as you can. You reach under your dirty clothes pile. That's where you keep Beto's bag hidden. You both traded backpacks long ago, for just this reason. For when you find yourselves out of the house and on your own, these "just in case" packs come in handy: extra clothes, toothbrush, toothpaste, other necessities. Last time you took off, you just decided to keep yours yourself. You figured you didn't need a middleman any more. You set your bag right out in the open, at the foot of your bed. In plain view, where no one would mistake it for anything other than a backpack. You learned that from a detective story you once read, real boring, but you took from reading what you could.

You pull Beto's bag free and turn. On your left is the bathroom, your very own, with its own door and its own lock. You spent the better part of tonight in there, locked in. Your mom had come home from her evening shift at the store, and your dad had been home a couple hours, drinking and doping up some. If you stayed in your room, kept the headset on, the music low, and studied, you'd most likely be okay. But you knew it wouldn't be a good night tonight, like any other night when he'd come home this early from his job, before your mom, and already messed up. So when you heard your mom walk in, you took off your headset, and waited. You paced up and down your floor, biting at your fingernails, knowing there'd come the explosion soon. And it did.

Your mom raised her voice to him, and your dad turned over the coffee table, screamed hard at her, "You flipping witch."

"Leave me alone, your dirty bastick," she answered.

Over the years, you'd taken to sanitizing their language in your mind, maybe doing so would clean up your memory of them, make you think you came from a solid, happy home. If you're honest with yourself, you have to say it isn't working.

Earlier you imagined your mom must've gone for the front door, because you heard your dad stomp heavy across the living room floor. Quick for a fiend and a drunk.

"Help, somebody help me! He's gonna kill me! Some-body call the cops! Anybody," she screamed.

Then the door slammed, next came the bump against the living room wall that was your wall too, so you heard it real clear and your picture frames shook a bit. No one called the cops tonight, or ever. The neighbors know bet-ter than to get involved. This is family business, like your neighbors' is their dirty laundry, and nobody ever wants nobody else sticking their fat noses in your goings-on.

So with all that racket, you turned the lock on your bedroom door, then took your books and several CDs into the bathroom and locked that door too.

You've seen the bruises on your mom the day after fights like this one. Scared stiff by them, scared plenty enough to learn to lock yourself in. You never study from the books you take in with you, really. Take them in there, you don't know why. You mostly cry instead, like tonight. And like all those other times, tonight you didn't come out until about two hours ago when you heard your parents' bedroom door slam shut, one last outburst, then they were out. You waited a little while to make sure, dried your eyes, and came to bed. Under the covers you'd been reading whichever Shakespeare play was the seniors' turn to read—*Macbeth? Julius?* What did it mat-ter? None of it was making sense to you. *Who cares about this stupid stuff?* you'd been thinking. This play was the fourth of Shakespeare's in as many years. You saw how good at playing with language he was, always hiding sec-ond and third meanings behind one word, but his stories always seemed alike to you, like American sit-coms: always the initial misunderstanding, someone hearing only the second half of a conversation, then the rest of the thirty minutes, everybody on the show going around like chickens with their heads cut off, then right before the end of the comedy, someone says something like "Oh, I thought he'd said such-and-such, not this-and-that." Everyone laughing it off then. Though there's more death in Shakespeare. You actually prefer his poetry. And tonight, you just couldn't get your folks' screaming out of your head, and the play you were trying to read was nothing but words jumbled. Then you heard scratching. It was Beto, and you were lucky for the break.

Now you have his bag. You can't decide whether to let him have the note you wrote to him the last time you ran. In it you tell him stuff you've never shared with anyone before, not even him. You decide it can't hurt to let him have it. You pull up on the screen and push the bag out at him. He shifts just so, so the bag won't boink him in the face, sideways kind of.

"Here it is," you say.

"Yeah, thanks," he says.

As he grabs the bag, he catches your hand too. His fingers are warm on your wrist now.

Last chance, you think. *Take back the note, or let him have it.* If he reads it, he'll know you're more scared than you let on. But you pull your hand away.

He leans in—what? To kiss you?

You say, "Listen, you gotta go. I've got more reading tonight. And you've got to figure out what you want to do."

"Yeah, okay. So where should I go?" He pushed the screen back in place.

Jessy stayed quiet a little bit, helped pull back the screen. "Man, Beto, there's places, but the best one, just to hang out temporary before really taking off, has got to be the recycle container over behind Concha's Grocery Store."

She filled you in on the details. It won't stink in there like the regular trash one, there's a spigot right behind the store to wash in the morning. It'll be a bit noisy sometimes if there's traffic, but the light's good, it's warm enough, but it's no hotel either. "Make sure you get up before morning shift comes in and starts with the trash, though. They don't care for that one bit."

She was quiet for a moment. Then she asked, "You gonna be okay?"

Beto wanted to say, "Why not come with me? We'll be a team." But instead he said, "Yeah. No worries."

And it must have looked like it to Jessy because she asked, "What?"

Beto took a chance with what was on his mind. "I got an idea: maybe you and me can head to San Antone together. Bonnie-and-Clyde-it, minus all the shooting? What d'you think?"

"Maybe not," she answered.

He must've looked sad to her because right after she said something about each having to go his own way, she quoted part of the poem by Frost about the road less traveled and added that with him along her path really wasn't her own.

"I want to be the first to take the road alone," she said. "See you at school tomorrow?"

"Yeah, I'll look for you at breakfast. Later."

He did notice that she'd pulled away from him when he tried to hold her hand and kiss her earlier. *Why'd she do that?* he wondered. *We've kissed before. Mostly playing around or daring one another. But tonight, just plain cold, that girl.* He wouldn't look for her in the morning. Most likely he'd be busy saying goodbye to some of his pals, making last-minute plans, snagging a map of Texas from the library, and the rest of the day just lay low.

Anyway, Beto had a place to go now. He left Jessy's and crouched at the foot of a telephone pole to gather himself, his thoughts, go through his bag. A towel, two T-shirts, some underwear, socks, but no shoes. He needed shoes. If he was going to school in a few hours and later be on his way, he needed them. He hooked the bag onto his back.

He decided to walk back to his house to get his tennis shoes. Maybe. Not if more than the porch light was on. That meant his dad was up still, or his mom, which would be worse because she'd be crying.

He jumped the fence again, saw all the lights were out, even the porch one. Beto felt his chest go like liquid, sloshing, heavy. No lights meant his dad had gone to bed and his mom, too, and Roelito. No porch light meant Dad thought Beto wasn't even worth trying to ward off.

He remembered he left his shoes outside his room. It'd be easy to snag them. He pulled his house key as quiet as possible from his pocket. If his dad hadn't latched the screen door he could pop it open it, but that would be too noisy. If he had to, he would skip school, which was an okay plan, too, since that was old hat and nobody'd miss him, except for the principal to chalk one more up against him, tell him he was flunking on account of truancy. Then he'd have to go to summer school or tell the principal, the teachers, the counselors, all of them, to shove that diploma, which was nothing but a piece of paper says you got educated. *Education*, Beto thought, *is overrated.*

And besides, he was a runaway now. Same rules of life didn't apply after tonight. Anyway, school was just a bunch of teachers who were way beyond boring, counselors too busy with paperwork to look out for kids with issues and principals who were no "pals" of Beto's. The security guys seemed like they were on the up-and-up, but Beto didn't know whether to trust them outright. They were part or the system, after all. Captain Bermea, the cop in charge of them, he was a real cop, had been a detective on the force in some town not too far away, changed jobs, was responsible for the high school and the three middle schools in the district. *But a cop's a cop*, Beto thought. *All part of the same organization.* Paid by the schools, so it was their interests Bermea was out to protect, not Beto's. How many times had this cop reminded Beto about how he was getting close to expulsion, about the gads of times he'd missed school and about the consequences? So Beto couldn't be too sure about even this guy.

Beto decided he had to show up tomorrow, make sure he made himself obvious to security, go to a couple of classes maybe, and, in that way keep under the radar.

Beto turned the corner, over where his and Roelito's bedroom was, and he heard a whisper.

"Beto, is that you?"

Beto stopped dead.

It was Roelito, his face scrunched up against the mesh of the screen.

"Beto, if it's you, say something. Pop's already gone to bed, Beto?"

Beto wondered if Roelito could hear his heavy breathing, his heart thumping hard. Beto kept still and quiet, just in case.

ROELITO—3:29 AM, March 27TH

I just know he's out there. I heard him.

"Beto," I say, "come in the house. I can go wake Dad up. We'll sit at the table, talk things out like we always do. I'll make some hot chocolate for us, thick and syrupy just like you like. It'll be a load off Mom, too. Come on in, B. What do you say?"

I'm quiet for a few moments, trying to hear him. I look at all the places I think he can be hiding: left, right, over by the trees, behind the car. But nothing.

"Beto, what happened tonight, you fighting with Dad. It's not such a big deal that you have to run away. We can talk it out and make it right. But you have to come inside. Beto."

Truthfully, I don't know if any of this is getting through to my brother. I don't even know if he's out there. It may be I want him to be there so much that I imagined he'd whooshed through the tall grass, shaken the fence jumping it and made those sneaking up sounds. I know this much: I don't like what happened tonight. I know a son isn't supposed to raise his hand to his father, much less push him around like Beto was doing to Dad, no matter how much your dad bugs you, how hard he rides you. A dad like ours, he only wants the best for us.

So what if he screams real bad at Beto sometimes? Beto does pretty stupid things to deserve Dad's getting after him. But my brother is a grown man, too. I can appreciate his side. Like he said to Dad not long ago: "If I wanted to, I could sign up with the military. I can vote.

You're the only one, Dad, who doesn't want to look at me like I'm a grown man already." So what's the big deal about him staying out late? Beto has never lied to me, that I know of, and when I asked him was he drinking and smoking like Dad says, Beto said, "No way, little brother, that stuff's for the birds. And I don't better catch you even thinking about trying any of that out. I'll slap you upside the head, get rid of your López good looks that way." Maybe Dad should be taking him at his word?

But still, a guy, one who wants to be thought of as a man, he can't be striking out at his father like Beto did. I just don't know who's right. I shouldn't have seen what I did. Should've just stayed sleeping. Ignorance is bliss, they say.

I don't hear a sound, so I say, "Listen, Beto, I may be talking to just the frogs outside, but if you're there, I want to tell you something. What you did tonight, man, it hurt Dad a lot. I heard him crying, telling Mom after you left. She was crying, too. Then she screamed at him. Said to him, 'You should know better than to push him.' Then they shut their door, and I haven't heard one peep." I don't tell Beto what else Mom said to Dad: "He's just a boy. My little boy."

"Anyway, if you're out there, I put your shoes and a clean shirt, underwear, and socks over by the tangerine tree. In the water bucket. Figured you could wear the same pants to school tomorrow. They're jeans, so no one'll know you're recycling, right? But dirty underwear, man, people can smell. Drop off the old clothes in the bucket and I'll put them in the dirty clothesbasket. I put some food out there, too. If you're not out there right now, well, there's all kinds of hungry animals who'll scarf it up."

Not one single noise, no movement toward the tree and the bucket. "See you in school tomorrow, bro?"

Nothing. "Well, you're not going for the tangerine tree, I guess. Not while I'm here at the window talking anyway. So I guess I'll go to the bathroom, then you can grab all your stuff. Later, bro. Miss you."

Miss *you, too.* Beto felt like crying.

He noticed the light in the bedroom come on and saw Roelito leave the room and shut the door behind him on his way to the bathroom, like he'd said. *I'm wasting time here.* So Beto ran for the bucket, grabbed whatever was wrapped in foil paper, his shoes next, and finally a brown paper sack. He punched everything in his backpack tight, then he made a run for the fence.

He'd gone a few yards in the alleyway when he stopped to put on his socks and shoes. Then he headed to Concha's like Jessy had suggested. He didn't want to think right now about Roelito or about what all the kid said. He wanted to get to the recycling dumpster, get situated, then maybe think about tonight: Go over every detail from beginning to end. He didn't know what to think about Roelito implying it had been Beto's fault what went on, like he was the only one pushing and shoving. Like their dad was some kind of saint. *No way!*

But thinking like that right at this moment was slowing him down, making him sluggish in the brain, wanting to stop, go back, and tell Roelito the way things really were. How for the last few weeks their dad had been on his case for every little thing. "A 'C' in English? How do you expect to get into a good college with punk grades?" "You're hanging out with who? And where?" "You think you're the big man now just because you can vote and shoot a man for the army?" On and on like that, it was a never-ending barrage of insults. A heap of nonsense was what it was. Beto was fed up finally. Had to break free. And if it meant fighting with his dad, then so be it.

Right now, he couldn't think of any of that. Didn't want to. Didn't need to. And every time something popped into his head, he slammed it back out. *Better to concentrate on the burning in my lungs, my wobbly legs.*

He neared the end of the alley again. Next he turned left into another alley, the one that would lead him right to the back of the grocery store. He could make out the two dumpsters up ahead. He had never paid attention enough to see them. One of them would be his bed tonight. Tomorrow he would have to find a better place. He wasn't trash. Or cardboard either—to be bundled up, tied together, and sent off to some center for recycling. He'd head to school in a few hours and ask around for a good place to bed down for a couple nights. Plan better, not so spur-of-the-moment like tonight was.

Beto slowed down a bit, took deep, deep breaths. His chest was on fire. He walked past the dumpsters, beyond the store, sauntered around the front of it, saw the night guy stocking soft drinks in the fridge. Nodded in the guy's direction to let him know he wasn't out to make trouble. Took the pay phone off the hook to make like he had a reason to be out in front of the store at this hour carrying a backpack. He hung up, then made his way to the back of the store again. He checked over his shoulders to be sure the coast was clear. He cruised real slow past the dumpsters again.

He could smell the regular dumpster, so he moved to the other one. He slid open the metal cover on the side of the recycle dumpster. At this hour, the noise seemed to Beto like it would wake up the neighborhood, metal scraping against metal. He scanned the alleyway, listening, but it was only dogs barking. He peered into the dumpster. Cardboard up about a quarter of the way. All the boxes cut or broken down and folded flat. He tossed his bag in, then took one last look down the alley in both directions. He didn't see anybody, so he climbed in and slid the cover back to where it was, slowly this time, so as not to make noise.

It was dark in there, and so he left the cover open a crack. He curled up into one of the corners and emptied his backpack. He hadn't eaten supper, so he chomped down on the ham and cheese sandwich and the chips Roelito put out for him. *He's such a cool kid.* There was also a bottle of OJ. He drank it in one gulp, cleared his throat, and the deep echo inside the dumpster stopped him cold. He listened for anybody who might've heard him. When nothing stirred, he bit into his food again. He was so loud swallowing his sandwich, and the crack of the chips was almost too much. He wondered if someone walking past could hear him eating. But he was too hungry right now to really care.

Finished, for no good reason, he cried like a baby. Why did he let his little brother see him fighting with their dad? Sure, guys argue all the time, fight even. And there's no hard and fast rule anywhere he'd read that kept men from fighting in spite of them being father and son. Hadn't brothers fought against one another during the Civil War? Killed each other? *Man, even in the Bible, the first brothers fought. One clubbed the other to death, as a matter of fact.*

But this was different. One, because this wasn't brother against brother but father versus son. Two, because he let Roelito walk right into the middle of it. There had to be a rule against that, written or not. He remembered he might have even whacked his brother on his side of the head, then just ran out on him. Roelito had asked him to come back, but Beto had been angry, too self-absorbed, careless. He heard the fear in Roelito's voice at the window—shaky and uncertain. What a jerk Beto'd been to fight with their dad.

Then there was the whole mess of his trying to kiss Jessy. And her rebuffing him. Still crying, he felt the cardboard under him shift to accommodate his weight, bent just so. He was so tired that soon after settling in he fell asleep, curled up in his corner.

CHAPTER TWO

March 27TH, Early AM

The three of them wake up within thirty minutes of each other this morning. Beto first when he's startled by a revving engine coming from somewhere near. Sometime later, Roelito when he hears his mother clinking around in the kitchen getting breakfast ready. Finally, Jessy when her alarm goes off.

They each get ready. Roelito and Jessy follow their usual morning routines, while Beto, for obvious reasons, has to think his way through this. But he manages, no need to go into the specifics really. This morning he slides the dumpster cover open several inches, and the light from the lamppost shines in on him. So even though it's still dark out, he can see better. He's rummaging through the bag, looking for breakfast and sorting out his clothes for today, when he notices something he didn't see last night. He pulls it free. It's a yellow envelope addressed to him in Jessy's cursive. He tears it open. It's a letter. He puts the paper to his face, and he smells Jessy. How'd he miss the bulky yellow envelope last night? It makes sense, though: he was out of it, to say the least, and it was much darker in the dumpster at three-thirty or four. It takes him a few minutes to get through the seven-page letter. After, he can't breathe right in here. He folds the letter and stuffs it into the book bag, then he packs up the rest of his stuff and jumps out of the dumpster. He's running. Again. And like last night, he doesn't stop. Lungs about to burst or not, he doesn't slow down until he gets to where he needs to be.

After getting ready and eating breakfast, Roelito kisses his mom on the cheek before leaving the house and hugs her just a bit tighter than normal. He doesn't say a word about Beto or last night. She doesn't either, but Beto, Sr. told her all that happened last night, even the part about Roelito stepping between the two of them, how he cried and begged them to shake hands like that would solve everything. She'd felt her whole life had been torn apart and cried the rest of the night. Today, she sees Roelito putting on a strong face for her. And so she does the same for him. She sees he's hurting. She's his mother, after all, and knows these things. As her baby walks out the door to head to the bus stop, she says, "You be good today." She wonders how long the day will be for her, for all of them, so she says a quiet prayer for her sons and her husband. She holds back a sob. Roelito's father has already left for work, but not before having checked on his youngest boy earlier. Beto, Sr. had stuck his head in the door and noticed Roelito had pushed his blanket from the bed. It lay crumpled at the foot. He saw the window had been left open and imagined his baby boy staring out of it all night long until he'd just slumped off to sleep. He'd have to talk to Roelito later on, maybe after work. Try to explain things. So with all of this, and his anger, sadness, and guilt from last night, he left for the day.

Jessy fixes herself breakfast, doesn't even try to pick up any of last night's mess, and instead just walks around it. In that way she's choosing to ignore it. Because if it doesn't exist, then perhaps neither do her parents. Her folks have either already gone to work or they're still in bed and will both have to call in to work to explain why they're running late this time. Or not show up at all. They'll lie to their bosses again, say that Jessy, their daughter, their baby had been ill last night and that they had to stay with her this morning, just to make sure she was okay before leaving for school. How many times had she overheard those calls? "But I'm on my way—be there in fifteen minutes, less depending on traffic," they'll each say. This will be the last time for Jessy's father to use her as his excuse. His manager will fire him within the week. Jessy grabs her books and begins her trek to the bus stop.

At the corner, where most of the neighborhood kids meet Monday through Friday to catch the bus, both Jessy and Roel search the crowd for any sign of Beto. They look away when their eyes meet. Instead of walking over to him and saying, "Morning," Jessy hangs back, talks chit-chat-nothing with some of the other seniors waiting on the bus. They're all pretty excited that they've only got a couple more months before graduation, how one is going to start university in the summer, another will take his basics at the community college, then transfer some-where, and that most of them are already getting "senioritis": "Our GPAs are pretty much set in stone, so who gives a flip?"

Jessy's got plans of her own, not any she wants to share with these punks, though. Her plans have to do with her leaving for San Antonio soon after getting that piece of paper. In San Anto, she'll study to become a painter. She's kept up on all the artistic goings-on there as written up in the *S.A. Express-News*. First thing every morning, she visits the library at school and reads that paper instead of either of the Rio Grande Valley papers that hardly ever say anything about the art scene. Jessy can't figure from these papers if there's a scene here at all or not. *So, why stay in this rat hole?* she thinks. *San Anto's where to be.*

The bus turns the corner and screeches, then lurches to a halt. All the students line up in a haphazard way, as though no one wants to be first on the bus. It's a lingering bunch, crooked and fat.

Jessy's already sitting when Roel spots her. The seat next to her is open, but the way she looked at him earlier, then away real quick like she did, she knows something, Roel thinks. *If I sit next to her, we'll both be uncomfortable, so why bother. She's likely not talking.*

It's obvious Beto's not on the bus, and both of them can only hope to see him at school. Roel realizes he's forgotten his algebra book. He slaps a fist into the palm of his other hand. Now he won't be able to look over the materials one last time before the exam.

The bus gets going, and Jessy and Roel search the neighborhood for any sign of Beto, but Beto's long gone. Has been long gone since after reading Jessy's letter and they're on the bus on the way to school, where there'll be *Macbeth* and an algebra test.

CHAPTER THREE

ROELITO—8:52 AM, March 27TH

"It seemed easy," Howie, my best friend says to me. "Don't you think, Roe?" It's only my family that calls me Roelito, little Roel. My friends call me Roe. Howie and I are standing out in the hallway. I'm scanning the length of it for Beto. No sign of him, though.

Without really thinking about what Howie's jabbering on about, I say, "I don't feel too good about it, man. I didn't get too much sleep last night. I just don't know."

Howie slaps me on the back. "That's what you always say, Roe. Then when we get our grades, you always score the highest. So don't sweat it. I'm the one that's got to worry. Aren't people supposed to have done bad when they think the test was easy?"

"We'll see," I say, all curt, meaning to cut him off.

I mean, really, who cares right about now? I certainly don't.

I want to know if Beto made it to school, learn if he's okay. Then give him a piece of my mind.

Last night, I thought I'd heard him out in the yard, so I asked him to come in, so we could talk through the situation around the table, the two of them, Dad and Beto, and me. What a stupid idiot I was, begging him: "Please, Beto, come inside. We'll work this out. I'll make chocolate, syrupy, just like you like it." *Idiot.* And how many times did I ask if he was out there, and if he was, to let me know? Like a million. Almost crying like a little girl. But he didn't make a sound. So I figured I was talking to nothing but shadows.

This morning, though, the bucket was empty. No clothes, no food. And that's the thanks I get. He was out there all that time and let me go on and on like a fool. "Please, please, please, Beto."

I don't even know if he's in school, and why should I care? Still, I won't go check with his teachers because how is it his own brother is oblivious to his older brother's whereabouts? They'll think it's suspicious, and the meddling will begin. They'll buzz the office and ask Maria about it.

Maria takes care of attendance, and I could check with her, but she's got her office almost next door to the principal's, which makes her part of that group. And then the prying will take on a more official intensity.

I could ask Jessy all nonchalant if she's seen Beto. But I don't even know where Jessy hangs out between classes. There was that look she gave me this morning at the bus stop, too.

I just don't know what to do. And still, punk that he's being, I can't get out of my head that I want to know Beto's okay.

"Listen, Howie, I've got to go. See you later."

I take a long look down the hallway. Nothing but a crowd of students ambling along to their next classes. I jump into the mess of people.

"You mean you're not going to English? You're playing hooky? If so, I'm with you. We'll make a day of it. Who needs to know about commas and stuff anyway?"

I turn and see Howie smiling big and lopsided, his hair falling over his right eye. He's right beside me, walking. Like I said, Howie's my best friend. We go way back to the beginning of middle school. We met in Chess Club. He beat me on our first game in four moves. I told him, "Try it again." And he did. Twice, actually. I couldn't figure out what he was doing until he showed me. After that, we didn't use that move on each other, but tried different ways to beat each other.

Best friend or not, right now I don't need him in my business. What could he know about my problems? At home it's just his sister Carrie and him, and everybody in his family loves each other. They never even argue the times I'm over to hang out. Real opposite of us.

"Naw, man," I tell him. "I just have to drop by the office fast. I'll get to class a little late, but you're right: Who needs commas and stuff?" I wave and leave Howie where the halls intersect. Then I head for the gym. That's Beto's second period. I just need to see for myself that he's all right.

CHAPTER FOUR

JESSY—7:37 AM, March 27TH

When you first get to school this morning, you head directly to the cafeteria where Beto said he'd meet you. You wait a good fifteen minutes and when he doesn't show, you make your way to the library. Like usual, you grab the *Express-News* from the rack and sit at your spot, over behind the chest-high shelf, at the little table for one. You try reading it, but it's no use. The mess your parents left behind in your head from last night's fight is bothering you big time. As much as you've tried to erase it from your memory, it's a heavy load on your shoulders. Even now, the images run scattershot through your brain: the vase your mom had bought three weeks ago was busted, the plastic flowers strewn all over the floor; the one photo of the three of you was also knocked off the coffee table; other stuff. You know your dad could've cared less to pick it up, but your mom hadn't either. And it hurt to see the three of you on the floor looking up, smiling. If they didn't care about picking it up, then why should you care?

So out of sorts, you decide to leave the library. See what you can see. You still don't know what to think about the letter you put in Beto's bag. What'll he think when he reads that you're scared every day, of just about everything, and not anywhere close to being the tough chick you want everyone to think?

So, with Beto's visit last night, the letter and your parents fighting like they did, your concentration's off, to say the least. Never mind Beto's almost-kiss. He's a good kisser, the couple times you both have tried that, but partway through you always end up laughing. You've never thought of him in that way, and you still don't, but what was he thinking? He knows where the two of you stand. You've been upfront with him, that you aren't interested in any relationships right now, not with him or with anyone else. You have plans, and anything like that will stop you short, way short. He shouldn't have put you in that position last night. You had to push him off. He had to get the message, no beating around the bush. You have yourself to look out for, and sure, you wanted to help him out, but kissing wouldn't have solved anything.

You need to freshen up, so you head to the girl's restroom.

Your focus is so off, though, that it isn't until you look at yourself in the mirror that you notice the little bit of eyeliner you applied that morning is running down your face. You have no idea when it was that you started crying, no clue if anyone out in the halls saw you boo-hoohooing like a baby.

But that doesn't matter either. What do they care that your life is what it is? Nothing! They have their own lives to worry over. You take care of yourself, and that's plenty enough. Even if others do see you crying, they won't say a word to you about it, won't poke fun at you. Not to your face. They're afraid to. You're tough and hard, right? Keep to yourself mostly, except for Beto. All the others know about you is surface information: you don't put up with anything from anybody, not students, not teachers, not principals. They just like to remember the time you told off the assistant principal. Even poked him in the chest, and he backed up, then noticed students looking and beginning to laugh, and he grabbed you by the arm real hard, though you wrenched free and spit at him. You were suspended for a week. When you came back to school, everyone stayed clear of you. What they didn't know then and don't know to this day is why you did what you did; and the assistant principal wasn't telling. The day you spit at him, he had said to Chela, your skinny neighbor with all that hair and makeup, that if she wanted to find herself a boyfriend, maybe she should learn to put on that face of hers right, go to one of the makeup places at the mall and ask for some help. She ran off crying. But you'd heard his crack and went up to the jerk. You weren't so tough really. But somebody had to stand up to bullies like him. He had no right to talk to Chela that way. To nobody, for that matter.

You hear the bell ring for first period, so you clean yourself up in the mirror, try on a smile, but it's so not you so you wipe it off along with your makeup. You take one last look and you head to English.

The last thing you want is any attention, so when Ms. García asks the class to turn to page whatever, you do it, even though you don't want to. You'd much rather be in the library reading about Chagall, this painter your discovered by accident last week. His stuff has this dreamy, floaty quality to it, and you want to figure out how he does it. Instead you're in English. Trying to keep it low-key. Trying to go invisible.

So wouldn't you know it, Ms. García calls on you. She never calls on you. Never! But today of all days, she does, and you're caught off guard. You don't have an answer for her. You're stumped, and you must look it because Ms. García asks you again about the reading for today, and you lie: "I didn't read the assignment," you tell her. "Anyways, Shakespeare's overrated." Thinking, hoping that'll shut her up and leave you alone. But you can't leave it at that. You say, "He was a punk, a dead, white playwright, who wrote some cheesy, fantastical trash. Who needs him?"

"Excuse me?" she says from behind her lectern. "I'm sorry to hear that you feel that way." The other students keep quiet, waiting to see whether Ms. García's going to get the Jessy treatment. She starts to walk away, but then turns and looks you directly in the eye: "Who needs him? I'm surprised at you, Jessy. Of all my top students, you should know better. He's not a dead, white punk, as you call him; he's, bar none, the best playwright of all time. He's endured this long because he got at the truth like no other writer. We can learn a lot from him."

For some reason you just can't control yourself. You know you should leave it alone, but you whisper, "You like him so much, stuff him." As soon as it leaves your mouth, you regret it. You hope she won't hear it.

But she does hear you, and that's when she says, "Jessy, can I see you outside, please."

You notice her voice quaver, and you feel rotten to the core. There's absolutely no reason why you have to talk like you just did to Ms. García. She's never done anything to hurt you, is the only teacher who thinks of you as a top student and says it in front of others, as a matter of fact.

She closes the door behind you, and you see she's shaking. You can't help but wonder if it's because she's heard the same stories about you as everyone else has.

She's quiet for a few moments, the whole while her eyes fixed on yours, and you decide this is what it must mean when all those writers describe someone's eyes welling up with tears. And she's not saying anything still.

You think, *Here it comes. All this quiet can't be good. I'm in it bad now. She'll send me to the office, then the office will call Dad at work, he'll curse me on the phone, then beat on Mom tonight for raising me the way she's done. I'll lock myself in my bathroom like always.*

Then you stop thinking altogether. Something doesn't feel right. You look away for a second, confused and you don't know why. Then you raise your face back again, and in that moment, things have changed. From the silence between you and Ms. García, the tears running down her face now, and you swallowing wads of breath you realize you've been telling her all of this the whole time. You hadn't been thinking any of that stuff, but saying it aloud instead.

Ms. García, crying for you, with you, wraps her arms around you, and breathes, "Shh, shh, now Jessy. Everything'll be just fine."

You wish it could be true, but you know the score.

She holds your hand while she knocks on her neighbor's door. "Mr. Saldaña, can you watch my class for a while? Jessy and I have to take care of some things," she says and nods toward you.

"Not a problem," he says. And the weirdest thing: you see his eyes watering up too, not enough to call it crying, but like he feels your heaviness, or feels Ms. García's and through her, yours.

Weirder still, you don't feel so alone right then. And Beto pops in your mind. You hope he's okay.

CHAPTER FIVE

ROELITO—8:59 AM, March 27TH

*W*here's my brother? I wonder. *P.E.'s the place he should be this period.*

I glance over all the faces in the gym again without giving away I'm scanning the area on purpose. I don't spot him, but I don't let it upset me so much because he likes skipping this class. That's part of why he's a senior and still taking P.E. with freshmen: he plays hooky, flunks, and has to start all over. He likes to joke that he's on a first-name basis with all the coaches, and that he's got his own office in the gym.

I turn to leave, but Coach calls out to me: "Little López, where's your brother? He's a no-show, again. Go figure."

I say, "Home, sick, Coach." But think, *How should I know where he's at?*

Then he says, "Tell him, he misses any more days, I'll be seeing him again next year. He'll be the only two-time senior doing jumping jacks with the kiddos."

Tell him yourself, I want to say. But I keep my mouth shut, still have several more weeks of my own P.E. class to go. I don't want the hassle, and I need to keep up my GPA. I don't like him thinking I'm Beto's messenger boy, though. I don't want to be Little López either, like I am who I am because of Beto. My brother's cool, and I'd be stupid not to want to be cool like him, but I'm my own man. And after what he did last night, I don't know how much I really want to emulate him. As far as standards go, my older brother has dropped a few rungs.

Now that I'm thinking about it, at home I've got a similar problem. I don't want to be Roelito. I've tried explaining my feelings to my dad a couple times. He grabs me in a bear hug and says, "You're the big man now, too big to be your old man's little man?" He calls me Roel for a couple hours, then it's back to Roelito.

So I wave to Coach and leave. Then I run into Captain Bermea over by the cafeteria where I'm checking next for Beto. And now *he's* about Beto, too. Like they all can sense when he's not around. Maybe things are calmer when he's not here? A kind of disturbance in the Force, like Star Wars? I tell him the same I told Coach: "Something like the flu, I guess. Had the sweats all night, aching bones. Shivering even under the covers." I can't believe I'm lying. Worse, I can't believe I'm this good at it.

I should just tell him the truth. He's always looked out for me and Beto, especially Beto. That time several guys had planned on beating up on Beto, the captain told my brother he was starting a new program. He'd take a chosen few, one at a time, on his rounds. Spend the whole day with him, see what they could learn. Beto just happened to be top of the list. Kept those guys from beating on Beto. Over the next few weeks, to keep up the show, Bermea actually took out a few more students.

"*Pobrecito*, your brother. I hope he gets better." Captain Bermea says, sarcasm dripping from each of his words. He starts walking away, then turns back to me. "*Oye*, López. So if I call home to check up on his health, is it your mom or dad who'll answer? I need to tell them he can't be missing school no more, sick or not. Word is he's not going to pass almost any of his classes this semester if he misses too many more. Won't graduate with his class. I mean, his new class. Anyway, I understand that maybe he'll have to do summer school again, and who wants to be in school in the summer? I know I don't need him on campus in the summer." He chuckles.

"You can try calling, Captain. But my mom this morning, she said something about maybe taking Beto to the clinic. So maybe she's home, maybe not." *Why do I have to lie?* Now he'll call and my mom will answer and what then? I have no clue. And I've still got three more years to keep my nose clean with the captain.

Man, Beto's something else, making me lie for him, and now Mom having to worry about him not graduating on top of what he did last night. But these guys, none of them—not Coach, not the captain, not anybody—needs to know our private business.

I start back down the hall toward English class. I wonder how much of today's reading I've missed.

"López," calls the captain.

I look over my shoulder as I'm walking away.

"I've got to ask: What are you doing out wandering the halls?"

"Nothing. I'm headed to English right now."

"Make sure you get there quick. I don't have the time to worry about the next generation of López boys. Got me?"

"Cool," I say, wave, and split. *You don't have to worry about me,* I think. More and more I want to be less and less like my brother.

CHAPTER SIX

BETO—5:09 AM, March 27TH

B eto recognized Jessy's handwriting on the envelope addressed to him, so he tore into it. It was a letter. He unfolded the several sheets and read. In it, Jessy told him one of the last times she ran away, she hadn't gone far—just over to a wooded area at the end of the fields. But she couldn't go through with it. She couldn't think of leaving her mom alone with this man. Things had gotten worse, though. The fighting had gotten nastier. It had begun to affect her more than ever. So she took off again. She was at the end of her rope, the threads of it unraveling real fast, the tiny loose threads fraying. She couldn't take it anymore, her parents' fighting, her having to lock herself in her bathroom because maybe next time her father . . . well, she didn't want to be his next punching bag, or worse: "I can't even go there in my mind right now," she wrote. "So I decided once and for all, this time would be it. I'd take off for real. No one would think I had it in me to go that far, right? I'd be just a wanna-be runaway, like the last six or so times, then I'd show up again. But not this last time. I'd made up my mind I wasn't coming back. I had it all figured out: I had the cash to head for San Antonio, find me a place on the cheap, right, and paint, paint, paint."

That's what she'd always talked to him about; both her immediate and long-term goals, she said, were to become a painter in San Antonio. She was good, too. She kept it mostly to herself, but the times they'd hung out after school in her room, Jessy'd shown him some of her work. His favorite was a wall-sized Pegasus/unicorn-combo flying across a dark blue sky. She had it hidden behind a curtain she'd tacked to the wall, but man, she was good. He told her so several times, and this morning, reading that letter, he thought it again. He also liked her portrait of him. He'd sat for it over a few days, after school, then he'd leave right about the time Jessy's dad was due to get home. Beto had sat as still as he could, embarrassed at being the center of attention this way, and she'd sketch from one angle, then move closer to or farther from him, to his left or right, "to get another perspective of you," she'd said during one of their sessions. "There's just so many ways to look at you, you know that?" Beto smiled at that, and she said, "See? One little move like that, a slight smile, and I've got to start over." He'd liked what she said: there were levels to him, and he only wished his dad could look at him like Jessy looked at him.

If only his dad would let him be his own man; instead, Dad was nothing but a hassle, constantly looking over his shoulder, like he was a *mocoso*, some snotty-nosed punk kid. It had really hurt Beto the one time his dad said, "Keep this up, and you're miles away from becoming a real man. Talking the talk is one thing; walking it is something else altogether. You're a good talker, *m'ijo*."

"I was ready, man," Jessy'd written. "I hitched a ride to McAllen, where I could catch a bus to the big time. I got to the station over on 15th and Austin, and it was nothing but noise everywhere and fumes, but the people were mostly quiet, kept to themselves, didn't look at anyone in the eye, waiting for their bus to show, people staring out across the street, but a blank stare, if you know what I mean. Tired, Beto—they all looked tired. And so was I. That's why I was running, right? And in line to get my ticket, it hit me, I was running away. I know we've talked about running away lots of times, but it'd never meant what it meant that afternoon. I was running not toward a place but away from *this* place—my life as it is. They would've won if I ran like this. So I hitched a ride back to Peñitas. Thinking very clearly now. It's only a few months till we finish with school, right, so why not stick it out? I mean, when it gets rough at home, and trust me, it's gonna get rough, I've always got my bathroom, right? Or better, I can crawl out my window and head over to your place. We can take off to the store, sit out on the bench, and talk about what we're gonna do soon." Jessy had it figured out.

Jessy's letter had made him wonder what his plans were. He had no clue; he had slept in a dumpster, for goodness' sake. He'd told Jessy, "Why don't we take off to San Antonio right now, the two of us?" But she'd said through the screen of her window, "No way, man, you got your own road to take, I've got mine. You'd only slow me down. And me you." *What had she meant by that?* he wondered. Wouldn't it be easier if the two of them did this together? Pool their cash, and together they could find a place easier, both of them working to pay the bills, the two of them on their own, but together. He wouldn't slow her down. He'd help her forward. He'd watch her back. Look out for her.

He kept reading: "As hard as we know it is, as scared as I am to feel so alone and little," she wrote, "we can't punk out now. We don't want to deal ourselves out before our hands are played out. Dropping out so close to the end—I don't know, I've got college plans, right? You've said you want more than what your dad's got, so I figure you've got ideas too. Quitting school now—well, it'll make getting started on those plans just that much harder.

"So if you're reading this, I guess you've taken off. I can't do or say anything to convince you I'm right. You have to discover that for yourself. Look at where you're at right now. Take a serious look around. On your own means *on your own* with no one to back you up. What you do is what you do. And nobody to blame for it. I'm sticking it out, ugly as it is. Okay, later, Beto, and take care of yourself. Your friend forever, Jessy."

Beto folded the letter and stuffed it back into the envelope. He heard more of the neighborhood noises outside. He didn't know what to do, where to go. Jessy said in her letter that in the end there was no place really to run to, that running away was like quitting. He knew about that: he'd quit playing in the band to play football, quit football when it got too long, hot, and boring at after-school practice, and the coaches didn't want anything to do with him once he'd quit the one time, so basketball was out, and so was baseball. His own dad, even, had told him a couple times he'd get no where fast if he started something and quit again and again. "Nobody's going to hire a quitter. Then where're you at?" his dad had said often enough. *So, where to, then?* Beto wondered.

Beto got all his stuff together, climbed out of the dumpster, shook out the kinks in his legs and back, and ran for home. He just wanted . . . well, he didn't know what he wanted, maybe to take just a last look, maybe walk inside, see his mom over by the stove, give her a hug, maybe shake his dad's hand and apologize. Maybe not go that far right now, but just show up as though nothing had happened last night, let it hang out there, a heaviness, a thickness too hard to breathe but what choice did they have, they were a family, right? They'd have to take him back. He thought of a poem he read once that said something like, "Home is where, when the chips are down, they got to take you back."

But in a way, that would be like quitting, too. He'd started something by taking off last night. He'd stepped out into the unknown. Decided on purpose, as quick as it happened, to become his own man. That's what he was doing, taking off, headed somewhere, not running away like Jessy'd written. He knew mostly where he wanted to be and didn't need anyone telling him what he could and couldn't do. Not Jessy, not his dad. Nobody. No one bugging him all the time, looking over his shoulder, sniffing him for cigarette smoke or beer. He had to strike out on his own. Although he didn't have a real place to go, he knew for sure he wasn't just running away.

But could Jessy be at least a little right? I mean, Beto thought, *I do only have a couple more months till graduation. It's a free roof, meals, a bed. If she can put up with her life in that house, it should be cake for me.* So maybe he could go back? Wait it out? He'd just make it clear to his dad that he was serious about deserving to be treated like a man.

That was it, then. Beto would go home, but there'd be conditions. He'd say, "Just a little respect is what I'm after, or I'm out of here, and this time, for good. No second chance. No turning back." Things would have to change, he'd tell his dad. "Man to man, I'm telling you, Dad, I don't do any of the stuff you accuse me of. You can trust me on that. So all I'm asking is for an open curfew.

I'll keep out of trouble, but you've got to have faith in me. Anything else you want from me, it's yours. Give me just this one thing."

He ran toward home. He stopped running just before reaching their property. Like last night, he jumped the fence. Next, he hid behind the *esperanza* bush, its yellow flowers in bloom like little trumpets blowing. From there, he saw fumes coming out of the car's exhaust. Beto, Sr. liked to warm the engine by running it for about ten minutes before driving away. Beto couldn't see anybody in the car, but it was still dark. He figured his dad had turned the key, then run back inside the house to collect his lunch and thermos full of coffee.

It was the middle of the week. His dad would have been up already since four or so, getting ready for work. Beto, Sr. liked leaving as early as possible to deliver the paper and then get to his regular job working for a landscaping company. He's the one who hauled topsoil or mulch to different locations, was in one of the company rigs practically the entire day. Not a bad job for a guy who started out only last year mowing yards and trimming hedges after twenty-six years of working as an inspector at a clothes manufacturing company that laid him off along with nearly a hundred others. At this job, Beto, Sr. had started at minimum wage, but after a few weeks, the boss was paying him what he was paying the others who'd been there much longer, and promoted Beto, Sr. because a worker like him didn't need to be mowing lawns anymore. So the bossman gave him one of the air-conditioned rigs.

That's how Beto's dad was. Never satisfied with just the bare minimum on anything. A go-getter. So it was surprising to the family that after losing the other job, the old man spent a week moping around the house because there wasn't much for him to do. One of his coworkers had recommended he take a few weeks to rest, to figure out what was next. But at dinner one night, Beto, Sr. told the family, "*Estoy harto.* I'm up to here with this business. I need a job. I can't waste my life sitting around doing nothing." Within a couple of days, he'd scored the paper route. A week after that, the landscaping gig. That was Beto's dad for you, impatient, couldn't just spend some down time at home after being let go, not even a little time. And he was always pushing Beto to be the same way: "You need to be earning your own money, *m'ijo,* know what that part of being grown up is about, so why don't you get a job? Deliver the paper like I do." Beto respected the hard worker in his dad, but Beto was a different kind of man. He'd cross that bridge when he had to.

From behind the *esperanza* bush, Beto needed to be sure nobody could see him hiding. He didn't think he wanted to talk to his dad just yet, maybe after school, but he wanted to look at his dad, see if there were bags under his eyes, looked unkempt from tossing and turning all night. Beto wanted to know. His own face, especially under the eyes, felt swollen.

The sky was turning lighter. Beto was dead silent and could hear the car's motor running. Beto hadn't seen any movement, so he got out from behind the bush and walked across the backyard. He wanted to hide behind the tangerine tree and be closer to where the car was, get a better look at his dad when he came out of the house.

That's when the car door opened, and his father stepped out of the driver's side, craned his neck, and said, "*M'ijo?*" His dad took a deep breath, and it seemed to Beto that his old man held it. Beto was surprised. He wasn't expecting a face-to-face confrontation like this, not right at this minute. He saw that his dad's eyes were also swollen from not sleeping much, or at all, and his hair was all a mess. Beto forgot what he'd wanted from his coming here for a short moment.

"Hey, Dad. Ah, you mind if I come with you to work? Maybe just for the route, maybe the whole day?"

Beto, Sr. let go of that breath he'd been holding. "If you don't mind rolling and bagging the papers."

Beto nodded. They both got in the car and drove off.

They'd been gone a good half-hour, before either Jessy or Roelito left for school.

CHAPTER SEVEN

JESSY—8:37 AM, March 27TH

Ms. García holds you by the elbow all the way to the teachers' workroom. She says you can use the ladies' room in there.

"A little alone time," she says. "Take as long as you need."

You walk in and sigh. You consider locking the door, but you decide against it. No need to. No shouting going on in the next room, just the whir of the air-conditioning system above you. *What just happened?* you wonder. *Why'd I break down like that?*

Three-and-a-half weeks ago was the last time Jessy ran away. She took off on a Saturday morning. Both her parents were sleeping a messy one off again. And Jessy thought, *I can't take it anymore. I'm out of here.* She didn't take her book bag as usual. Instead, she packed a suitcase, an old one she'd found at a secondhand store on the cheap—big and angular with marbley-green, hard side panels. *A painter's suitcase*, she thought when she first saw it. But with all her stuff thrown in, it was on the heavy side. She banged down the hall with it, set it down with a thud on the kitchen floor, and knocked around louder than usual fixing a noisy breakfast. When she was done eating, she called down the hall, "Mom, Dad, I'm taking off," then yelled it a bit louder, but like before with them, no response. She left a note on the table, where she knew her mom would see it. "Okay, bye. I'll send you post-cards," the note read. She listened, then said to herself, "What wastes of space. I am so tired of this place." Jessy swung open the front door, slammed back the screen and started walking, suitcase in hand, all the money she'd saved up over the last several months in her pocket, and her plan.

She headed for the store where she'd either hop on the Valley Transit bus to take her to the station in McAllen, or she'd hitch a ride. She was a tough one, knew how to fend off creeps, and wasn't afraid of thumbing it around. But she wasn't stupid either. While waiting for the bus to show up, she studied carefully her would-be rides. No reason to hop in the first car that made itself available. No sense in making it harder on herself and getting into a car with a whack-job, or a greasy old man with wandering hands, or someone wanting to counsel her back into the whack-job of a life back home. She needed a ride, plain and simple, and here it came.

She couldn't have been but thirty-five, no older, Jessy figured. She colored her hair orange, bright orange, and shiny, and wore it poofed up like old women did, but on this woman, it didn't look so bad. She took good care of her fingernails too, Jessy noticed, had soft skin, smiled at Jessy on her way back from paying for her gas. The woman turned back around and said to Jessy, "You need a ride, hon? I'm headed to Brownsville. If you're headed anywhere in that direction, I can drop you off some-place?"

"If you don't mind," said Jessy. "I mean, if it isn't out of your way, I need to catch a bus in McAllen."

"Best I can do is drop you off at the 10th Street exit. I'm in a major hurry, can't go too far out of the way, traffic anywhere down toward the station would slow me down, and I'd lose my job. So if you're willing to walk or find another ride from the exit to the bus station, hop on."

Jessy nodded and smiled back.

"I'm your guardian angel today, hon. Put that monster in the back."

Jessy threw her suitcase in and climbed into the front seat. The car was baby blue and huge, a boat of a car, the type her grandfathers would've driven in their day, but it was clean, comfortable, and the air conditioning worked. Morning and already hot out.

"Then we're off," said the woman, whose name was Lydia.

"I'm ready," Jessy said.

And before Jessy could take a last look around, Lydia pulled onto the expressway and started talking right off about this job she'd taken two weeks ago carrying boxes of files back and forth for a lawyer in Rio Grande City, to court usually. Only, this morning he'd sent her to Brownsville, with express orders to "get there yesterday, and don't dilly-dally, Lydia. I know how you like talking." Some important case was going on there, and if she'd known she was going to have to drive this far for a job, then maybe she wouldn't have bought this big old gas guzzler, or at least she would've borrowed her brother's car, much smaller and economical than this monster. She liked that word, monster. And on and on, nonstop. So Jessy, if she had wanted one last look at home, didn't have the chance for it. No great loss, though.

Jessy liked Lydia. She thought the orange-haired woman with the pretty nails would've taken her all the way to the bus station if Jessy had agreed to go all the way to Brownsville with her and back, just to have someone to talk to. Jessy would've gone, too, but she had to get started on her journey. She also had places to get to fast.

Too bad, Jessy thought. *Lydia's way cool*. Not once did she ask Jessy, "Hey, girl, where you headed? What you running from?" Just on and on about her job, her brother, his latest love interest, pointing out spots she remembered from when she was a girl herself about the same age as Jessy. "But my, how things have changed. That used to be nothing but orange orchards there. Now look, subdivisions of all look-alike houses, or used car lots. What a waste."

And soon enough, Lydia was letting her off on the corner like she said. The light was red so it was perfect timing, she said. "No time for long goodbyes, Jessy-girl. You take care wherever it is you're headed. People are generally kind, but be smart about it. I know I'm speaking to the choir, but still." Then the light turned green, and Lydia was gone.

Jessy was standing on the corner where the toothless, homeless guy normally held out his "Hungry, can you help me, thanks?" sign. He was nowhere to be seen today. She started walking north on 10th, dragging her suitcase behind her. On her left was the McAllen Convention Center. Past it down a ways Jessy could see the corner where the H.E.B. supermarket was, and across from it the Globe and Everything's a $1 store, and later, down from it, El Matador Motor Inn and a bakery, then the garage painted a bright yellow, a Pizza Hut across from it, and then a little farther down the bank that left office lights on during the holidays in the shape of a Christmas tree. She could see her path in her mind all the way down to Old

Highway 83. She'd turn left off 10th at Austin, just after
the bank, and head to 15th, where she'd eventually run
into the station, downtown old McAllen that looked and
sounded more like a Mexican downtown with the taco
stands, all the signs on windows in Spanish, and everybody talking the language, too.

But she'd only just now reached the end of the convention center, and the suitcase was getting heavier. Both
shoulders hurt from switching the suitcase back and
forth, and she was beginning to sweat. Why hadn't she
found one with the tiny wheels at the bottom so she
could pull it and not have to lug it around like this? With
one of those rolling suitcases, though, she'd look like the
Mexican nationals, the ones who come into McAllen
from all over the place in Mexico, pockets full of money
to spend, empty suitcases to be filled and plenty of shops
to visit at La Plaza Mall. So many of them stuffing their
merchandise in the suitcases, pulling them to the next
store, then the next, weekends at a time. They drive all
up and down 10th Street, and when they're done shopping, they pull into any parking lot and yank the tags off
their merchandise, stuff it all back into their suitcases.
Now when they return to Mexico, they look like they've
been vacationing, not shopping, and they don't have to
declare having bought near as much stuff as they've
bought, so as not to pay taxes that way and still expect
back money on their *manifiestos. Sneaky, sneaky, the
nationals*, Jessy thought, *but smart with the little wheels
on the bags.* Nationals were rude, to boot. Thinking that
just because they were spending cash here they could cut
in line at the registers, talk all ugly to the people working, who were mostly *pochos*, that is, Mexicans and Mexican Americans who'd abandoned their homeland, had

forgotten the culture and history, didn't know proper Spanish. Every chance she had, Jessy was rude back. She smiled right then because this Saturday morning, instead of driving, she was walking and carrying a clunky suitcase. She knew there was no chance she'd be confused for one of them. She still wished she'd found something with wheels, though.

She stopped off at the H.E.B. gas station when she reached it finally and pumped the soft drink machine with enough coins for two bottled waters. Not even on the bus yet and already spending her money. She should've packed some water from home. That would've been the smart thing. It was still early in the morning, and it was only getting hotter. She rested some under the shade, sipped at her water, then she was off again. She could've cut over to Broadway or 15th that ran parallel to 10th, but she wouldn't yet. She knew this street better. On 10th it was populated, busy. Those other streets she didn't quite know. *Better safe than sorry.*

Cars passing by, honking their rude horns at other cars also zooming past, turn signals going left and right, brakes screeching. All these people everywhere, and Jessy was on her own. Not getting one bit of help from anybody. Not asking for it either. Not needing it. But still, a person could offer. Then she remembered Lydia—she'd been a huge help. Without her Jessy'd still be back at the corner store in Peñitas. Maybe heading back home, her chin down so far it would be rubbing her chest. She didn't want that.

But the rest of these people driving up and down 10th, they didn't even look at her. She thought that was supposed to happen only in the big cities, the New York of the movies, Chicago, Houston, places where there were millions of people all vying for some elbow room.

McAllen wasn't nowhere near as big as those places, all kinds of elbow room here, more in Peñitas, so why didn't people look at each other?

No matter. After a few more pit stops under awnings or trees, Jessy reached the bank and read the time and temperature: 10:23 and 87 degrees. Soon it'd be sizzling. She wondered what the weather was in San Anto, a good three- or-three-and-a-half hours north from here. She cut through the parking lot. The bus station wasn't too far now. A block down on Austin Street, she saw an old ice-house. Across the street from the abandoned building and from this distance, Jessy knew they were murals, paintings that covered entire walls. In one, she could make out a female bust, bright green, and goddess-like. A door next to that, all of its panels covered in different designs. At the corner, a huge painting, part of a woman's face resting on her leg? Then the last one, three girls, all holding hands. *It's beautiful*, Jessy thought. She crossed the street and got up real close to the painting, first at arms-length, then just inches. It didn't look anything like it did from across the street. Jessy noticed the artist had used so many different colors and tiny strokes; from up close, it looked more random, like a colorful mess. She'd never seen anything like this in person. She studied the painting, wanted to learn how the artist had done what he did.

She heard a car braking to a stop at the corner. She so wanted to stay here, in front of the painting, to squeeze the life out of it. But time was passing. She needed to get going. So she took her suitcase and trudged off toward the bus station. All the way down the few blocks left, Jessy kept thinking, *That was beautiful. And go figure, something like that on a wall here in McAllen. Wow!*

When she got to the station, she found a place to sit and rest some, a bench just outside the terminal. The noise and the air quality were worse here than on 10th, with the constant drone of bus engines, the fumes to go with it, and the bustle of people wanting to go somewhere, or getting here from somewhere else, waiting to get picked up, many of them toting black trash bags for suitcases.

Jessy wondered how many of these folks wanted out of the Rio Grande Valley as much as she did. That's why they were here today, on a Saturday, instead of being home or at a park. She was sitting next to an old man wearing a tattered Atlanta Braves baseball cap. He was staring at nothing across the street, it looked like to Jessy. She thought she would try painting him one day, in the same style as the painting back at the icehouse. Something definite and sure from afar, but up close, a mishmash.

Directly in front of them, across the street from the station, was Hollywood Fashions, dresses that looked a little too hoochie for Jessy, showing off too much skin. To her right was a toy store, the New World. Plastic and shiny trinkets, all colors, all sizes, all made in China, most likely. So much was happening, but the man did not notice it, just sitting there, bored with life. *Where's he headed?* Jessy wondered. *Wherever it is, I'd rather not go there.*

Jessy heard some scratchy noise over the PA, and the man got up to go. He looked at Jessy, but in the same way he'd been looking across the street, all blank, like nobody looking at nobody and nothing. Jessy tried smiling at him, but he grunted something at her. She didn't want to go nowhere near where he was headed. Loserville. It seemed to Jessy, from his slumping shoulders, this man had no place to go. She tried to imagine what it was that had got that man to this point, what was it that caused him to close up this way. And it dawned on her: he probably started running early on, found out for himself it wasn't the place you headed to or from, but the place you were at inside yourself before you left. *And if you're in the wrong place inside*, she thought, *then nowhere you go will make it better.* Then, in line to buy a ticket, something else dawned on her: she wasn't thinking about the man any more, but about herself. She realized she couldn't leave yet. She wasn't done, actually.

She had only several more weeks left of school. Then she would march and get a diploma. She'd be legit, could make her own decisions as an adult, wouldn't have to run away from home, but leave it instead, head straight out, go to another place, the right way.

She decided she'd find her way back to her house. That's how she thought of it now, a house, nothing home about it, four walls of her room inside another four walls. Not even her mom helped out except to say, "Storm's coming. Lock yourself in." Well, she was done with locking herself in. She had to reenvision that whole business. Call it by another name. See it different. She wouldn't lock herself in, maybe lock others out. But that'd be just as bad. *Forget locks*, she thought.

Her house, she realized at the bus depot, was nothing but a way station, a place to sleep and eat, and in the meantime bide her time. A place to hang out waiting for the way out, waiting for the right time, and that time was right around the corner, only weeks away. She could do it, wait them out, stay out of their way. Just eat, sleep, and wait. Then the day would come. Soon enough.

She eventually caught a ride back from McAllen with a husband and wife headed for Sullivan City. When Jessy walked in, her mom was up and eating breakfast.

"Hey, Mom," she said.

"Where you been?" her mom asked Jessy. She didn't even notice that Jessy was carrying around the suitcase. Or if she did, she didn't say anything about it.

Jessy passed the kitchen on the way to her room, and she saw her note still where she'd left it. Later, her mom and dad left to the grocery store. Jessy went into the kitchen and took back her note, still in its envelope. *Soon enough*, she thought. *Soon enough*.

But it hasn't gone as planned, has it? As much as you tell yourself that it's mere weeks now, you still can't help getting scared every time your mom and dad fight, because, yeah, what has your mom been warning you against, but trouble. You're next in line. The man has to someday get tired of the old punching bag and look for a new one, and guess what? You'll be it. So for a few weeks now you've kept locking the door behind you, no matter what you decided at the bus station that day. But you're also locking those two people out of your life.

They don't care about you one bit, that's obvious. That day your mom hadn't even found the note, and it was right under her nose. Addressed to her in black marker. If they can care less, why should you bother about them? You haven't let it affect you. You've been cold, you've stared like that old man on the bench, but you know you're different from him. Countless times, you've recalled that painting of the three sisters, hands linked, their hair all wild. You've even gone back a couple of times to the icehouse to study it some more. Wondered who painted it. Was she, or he, doing more stuff, just like this, and how could you find out? You've even started doing your own paintings like it. Of the old man wearing the ball cap, all the commotion on the streets that day, the busses arriving, then leaving, men and women, all their belongings in black plastic trash bags or falling apart suitcases. No one smiling, every one of their faces blank. You've wondered if any of them tried painting you, would they find your face just as cold and blank? No. Yours is only a temporary coldness. It'll last just a few more weeks.

But then last night, your parents went at it again with the screaming and the beating on each other. Then Beto came up and he must have seen how your eyes were inflamed and puffy, but he didn't ask about how you were doing, just wanted to know the way out, wanting to leave together with you, mess up all your plans. You were tempted, but quickly shoved that thought out of your head. Then to top it off, he wanted to kiss you.

And it's all come crashing down on you this morning. Strong or not, it all caught up to you, and you cried.

And you're crying again in this bathroom in the teachers' workroom. Outside you feel Ms. García pacing. *Maybe she's crying again, too?*

Then Ms. García knocks on the door. "Are you okay, Jessy?"

You wipe your face, look at yourself in the mirror, and say, "Yeah, thanks. I'll be just a second."

"Never mind about that, Jessy. You take all the time . . . " and she breaks up.

You ask yourself, *How can this woman be crying over something that's not really her business? I mean, I ain't her daughter, just her student?*

Collected, you open the door, and Ms. García isn't crying anymore either. She's standing there in front of you, and she takes your hand again. How great that feels to you. "You want to talk to somebody? The counselor? The nurse?"

"Nah," you answer. "I'm okay."

And oddly enough, you are. You squeeze her warm hand in yours to show her you're on the up and up. It's just all run together too hard at you, and you couldn't keep it all in, you tell her. This cry from this morning has been good. A release.

"Thanks," you tell her, squeeze her hand again like she had yours, and you smile.

It takes her a few moments, but eventually so does Ms. García.

This'll make for a good painting, you think. From across the street it'll be of two women, arms wrapped around each other, crying maybe. In the up close mess, though, if people look careful enough, they'll see splotches of paint that were their smiles.

CHAPTER EIGHT

ROELITO—8:17 AM, March 27TH

ike I figured, I didn't miss out on anything much coming in late to English. Mrs. Longoria has us reading through the cartoon version of *A Tale of Two Cities*. I don't get it. We're in high school now, so why are we looking at pictures and calling it reading? Something else I don't get is this story. If it's boring as a comic, I can only imagine how much of a drag the real book is.

"This is an abridgement, that is, a shorter version of one of my all-time favorite novels," explained Mrs. Longoria when we first started with this "book" last week. "Charles Dickens is among this world's best writers . . . ," and on and on she went.

Eventually the bell rings and I'm off to lunch with Howie. On the way, he wants to know why Beto's not been in class. I think it's weird that Howie's interested in my brother's whereabouts, but I don't have the will to put on a show. Instead, I tell him, "Don't worry about it. None of your business anyway."

"Oooh, Mr. Rude-man."

That's one thing wrong with Howie: he never takes things seriously, always exaggerating.

"Just showing some concern. It's my sister, Carrie, actually who wants to know, really. Before English she found me and told me she didn't see him in class this morning. Just worried about him, I guess. I think she likes him."

We walk through the doors at the end of the hall, and we're in the patio.

"You think he'd be interested in her?" Howie asks. "I don't know—my sister and your brother? They just don't match up. I mean, yeah, my sister's all right looking, I guess, but she's on the straight-laced side, you know, Miss Goody Two-shoes. And your brother, well, I don't have to tell you about him."

What does that mean? Sure, Beto's a punk sometimes, but, what? Howie thinks his sister's too good for my brother? Maybe Howie thinks he's too good for me, then? "You know, Howie, you're right. You don't have to tell me about Beto. I know for myself. What's with everybody today?! 'Where's Beto? Is he sick? Oooh, poor Beto.' You all're getting on my nerves, man." I can't figure out, though, why it bothers me that Howie is bad-mouthing Beto.

"Ease up, Roe. I was just asking for my sister."

We're at another set of doors that lead into the cafeteria. On pizza days, like today, the end of the line reaches several feet out into the patio. Now I can call pizza day an unabridged lunch line day. Normally I'd share smart jokes like that with Howie, but not today. He's being a jerk, can't see my mind's on more serious stuff than hooking her sister up with my brother. I think I maybe want to tell him what all is happening with me. He is my best friend, after all, but right now he's got me going on this other thing about defending Beto when, really, I probably think the same, if not worse, about him.

Instead I say, "What are you? Your sister's messenger boy?" I stop well before the doors and turn to Howie. "Is that what you are, an errand boy?"

I push myself into him; we're right upon each other, chest to chest practically.

He can't look at me. He's looking at something to his left in a flower patch.

"Okay, errand boy," I say and shove him back a bit. "You can run this one for me," and I intend to tell him to go get two lunch trays for us while I find us a place to sit, but he takes a wild swing at me.

I duck out of its way, surprised he's even tried to take a whack at me. "Whoa, there, Punchy," I say, laughing at him. "You don't want to start something like that."

He swings again, but he's too obvious, telegraphing it's coming because he's punching like in the movies, all dramatic, cocking back his arm, like saying "Here it comes now." He misses a second time, and now he's so angry, he's all red in the face and beginning to shake. He's getting teary-eyed. A few people look our way, some of them laughing. *Serves him right, thinking he's better than me.* Although it bothers me that people are laughing at him because of me.

I say, "That's enough, Howie. You're making a fool of yourself. Stop it already. Oh, and when you talk to your sister, tell her you punch like a girl." I mean it jokingly, but Howie doesn't get it that way. He just gets angrier.

I don't see the next one coming. His fist catches me square on the nose, and I stumble backward and almost fall except a column gets in my way. Through the stars, I see he's in my face now.

"You're a punk, man," Howie says and walks away.

"Hey, man," I say, "lucky shot," worried someone may have seen all that just happened and is laughing at me now. "You still hit like a girl."

He waves me off and keeps walking.

I am a punk, though, and I feel bad because I know Howie's family's on the poor side, and he really looks forward to his free lunch at school. And I'm making him walk away from pizza today, his favorite. I'm such a big dope.

I get my bearings and get in line. I still don't look around, making like I didn't just get popped and almost fell back. I rub my nose till it hurts. *What's with Howie?* I didn't mean anything by it. The guy just can't take a joke. Anyway, he just wouldn't stop bugging me about Beto, even after I told him I didn't want to talk about it.

"López."

I look around to see what teacher's calling me now. It's Mr. Ramírez, my Algebra I teacher. I wonder if he saw the punch and is now going to turn us into the office for fighting.

"Listen," he says as he puts one hand on my shoulder and sticks the other one out for me to shake. I can't leave him hanging, so I take his hand. It's a hard grip he gives me. He's smiling. "I'm done grading most of the exams from this morning, and it's no surprise, you scored the highest in your class. I'll be surprised if you don't score the highest from all my classes."

We're not shaking hands anymore, but he's still got me by the shoulder. He pulls me out of line. "Let's talk over here," he says. People around us are beginning to stare.

"But, sir, I'll lose my place." I'm way at the very end of the line, but still. They could run out of pizza if this takes too long, if even a few more people take my spot in line.

"Never mind about that right now. I'll walk you to the front in a sec, okay? This is more important."

The front? That sounds like a solid plan. So I go with him.

Even though he just told me I passed and I worried for nothing about flunking because of Beto last night, I'm nervous. Teachers never kid around when they say "This is important." It's like the folks sitting you down and saying, "Son, we've got to talk." It's got to be trouble I'm in.

We're standing face-to-face now. My nose is aching.

"I'll be honest, López," Mr. Ramírez says, "when I found out at the beginning of the school year that you were Beto's baby brother, well, let's just say I would've given anything to drop you from my roster. I shouldn't be saying this," he says, but whispering now, like we're buddies. "But I don't care for your brother one bit, that's how much a troublemaker he was when he took my class. And I figured you were a chip off the old block. You looked enough like him, you had to be like him too. Worse, maybe."

I'm quiet the whole time, listening. He's right, I do look like my brother, even dress like him. When he lets me, I wear Beto's Yankees baseball jersey. I even comb my hair like him, slicked back with gel. I want to tell Mr. Ramírez not to worry, I'm nothing like Beto, but the man's talking about my brother, my family. But the man is also the person with the grade book and the red pen, and someone in my way of pizza, so what's he up to, talking to me about Beto like Beto's a disease? I listen.

"Well, you've proved me wrong; you're nothing like your brother. You don't know how relieved I am. Anyway, I'm sponsoring the UIL Math team next year, and I wanted to invite you to be on it. It'll be mostly seniors and juniors, so you'll be low man on the totem pole, but you're good enough, I can tell. What do you say?"

I shake my head. I don't know what to say, so I tell him so. I don't tell him I don't like him talking about my brother. He's right about him for the most part, but still.

"You're right. Think it over, but I'll tell you what, membership in an academic team can only help when you start applying for college. And as early as you can, you've got to start thinking about that. Most seniors don't think about college till the last second, much less when they're freshman, but the competition's more fierce today than it was in my day. Getting in is cutthroat, so the sooner you start getting ready, the better."

I want to tell Mr. Ramírez he's old news. I've already narrowed my choices of universities to the top five, and I have a list of another ten as fall-backs. I don't mention it, though. I don't know Ramírez except as a teacher, and he doesn't know me. Ramírez is looking right at me and me back at him, but I'm thinking Beto knows what my top five universities are. He even took a Saturday afternoon once, sat with me, read through that mammoth university guide and quizzed me about all the places I'd highlighted. Said to me, "You need to look for a place where there's *raza*, so you don't have to look over your shoulder all the time. Brown around you is a good thing." He thought it was hilarious that I'd chosen Brown University as number four. But Beto's never talked about himself going anywhere. And so what if he gets on Ramírez's nerves? He gets on everybody's, just a rub-you-the-wrong-way type.

"Let's go," Ramírez says, and he leads me to the front of the lunch line. "Think about UIL Math. No hurry. It'll be a good experience. Plus you'll get a better letter of recommendation from me if I've got more good to write about you."

"Yeah, I'll let you know," I tell him and grab my lunch tray. *Recommendation letters?* I hadn't even begun to think about them.

I spot Howie sitting over by the lockers. He's biting his fingernails. He does that when he's nervous mostly. I guess he does it too when he's upset.

"Howie, how's it going?"

He looks up at me from where he's sitting. "You didn't get enough of making a fool of me earlier? Or do you want some more of this?" he says and balls up his fist. It's swelling up and red at the middle knuckle. "Don't you know when to quit?"

And that's my problem, I don't know when to quit. That's another way I'm different from my brother. He quits band, football, church youth group; quits caring about Mom and Dad, about me, about himself; quits being a cool brother to me. I'm not like that.

I say to Howie, "You don't know how sorry I am, man. It's just . . . well, first, how about some pizza? But I get the bag of chips. You get the milk. I bought a can of Mountain Dew for myself. I need the sugar rush. Rough day." And it doesn't even dawn on me that I'm the one who got punched in the nose so who should be apologizing to whom? I just know I'm real sorry and I can't lose my best friend on top of everything else that's gone wrong.

"You mean, all this time I've been out here and you're just now getting your lunch? Or are you setting me up, trying to pass off some cold pizza?" says Howie.

"No, it's still hot. Feel for yourself," I say.

He sticks two fingers into the tomato sauce, cheese, and pepperoni. An old trick of ours: when we want to call germy-dibs on something like food, we stick our greasy fingers into it thinking the other'll be so grossed out he won't touch it. Usually works.

"You're right, it's still good. What then? You spit in it?"

I'm paying for it now. But that's cool. I deserve it.

"Naw, man. It's like a peace offering. I'm really sorry I talked to you the way I did. It's just . . . last night wasn't a good night at home."

I want to go on, tell him everything that happened with my dad and Beto, but it doesn't want to come out. I can't say a word. Thinking about it makes my eyes tear up, so I can only imagine I'll start crying like a girl if I tell him more.

"It was bad is all I can tell you right now, and it has to do with Beto. So when you, and Coach, and Captain Bermea, and everyone else and their grandma was asking about him, I just couldn't take it. You're my best friend, man. And I shouldn't have talked like that to you. The peace pizza's solid. Trust me."

"How about I get the soda and you take the milk? Then we'll be okay."

"I don't know that I'm that sorry," I say, but, *Sure*, I think, *why not? What's a can of soda if not something to give to your best friend?* I pop the tab on it, take a swig, and pass it off to him.

"Oh, you'll never guess why I really took that long in line," I say.

"What?" he says.

I tell him about Mr. Ramírez's offer to join UIL Math, leaving out the Beto part.

Howie perks up. "That sounds great. I was thinking of joining the Ready Writing team. Now we can go to meets together. Cool." He's quiet for a second, then takes a drink. "How's your nose?"

"Not bad." I pinch it to show him. "I don't mean to beat a dead horse, man, but like I said earlier, you hit like a girl."

I don't tell him that my nose really smarts. There wasn't any blood, so I'm thinking it can't be broken. But there were stars.

"Yeah. That's what you say, but I almost knocked you out, man."

I try to laugh it off. So does he.

"Roe, you're not the only one who's got it hard, whatever it is you're going through. I just thought as your best friend I could help."

"Yeah," I say, but leave it at that.

CHAPTER NINE

JESSY—8:47 AM, March 27TH

"**J**essy, it'll be just to talk it over with someone who's a trained professional," Ms. García tells you. She wants to send you either to the counselor or the nurse. "That's what they're there for, Jessy. To listen."

What Ms. García must not know is that by law, she's required to report to the proper authorities what you've confessed to her. What you told her earlier would probably be considered an emotionally abusive situation by children's protective services. Once they're involved, it becomes a whole different mess. A distraction for you, really. At this point anyway. With under two months of school till graduation, you've already decided you're going to stick it out and then take off to San Antonio, diploma in hand, not a dropout. You're no runner, no quitter.

And although they all mean well, they'll only mess things up for you right now. You're not a child anymore, right? The time you were suspended for standing up to the assistant principal was the last time you were in the real principal's office, and he told you, "Jessica, you're a young woman, not a little girl. You need to start behaving like it." Back then you thought you were acting like an adult. Still do. The assistant principal told his boss only part of the whole story, left out what he'd said to Chela. You didn't rat him out, either, because you thought that's not the way adults behave, right?

Well, here you are again, trying to behave like an adult. Earlier this period in front of Ms. García was nothing more than a mini-breakdown. Who could blame you, really? You've been under some stress at home, to say the least.

If Ms. García gets her way and you head over to the counselor, then the counselor is obligated to call the authorities. You know this because something similar happened to your cousin, Laura, when she was in the fourth grade. Her teacher found her crying in the girl's bathroom during recess one day and took her to the nurse. When the nurse spotted a bruise on her arm, she jumped to conclusions, started in on Laura about how "This office is a safe place. Here you don't have to be afraid of anything or *anyone*. And you know, it's my job to help anyone who needs it. Do you understand?" Laura nodded. "So," the nurse said, holding Laura's hand, "you can tell me the truth." The nurse wiped Laura's tears and touched the bruise. "Do your parents hit you at home?" She thought Laura's bruise had come from either her mom or dad, or worse, both, grabbing tight on her arm while hitting her or shaking her. This was the nurse's testimony in court over the next few weeks: "I just thought . . . and so it only made sense to me that . . . you understand," she argued. "My concern was for the little girl's well-being."

Laura didn't know this was how the nurse was thinking that day the teacher caught her crying in the bathroom. She thought the nurse didn't like kids getting spanked even a little. So Laura told the truth like she was supposed to: "Yes, ma'am, my parents spank me." Her parents, truth be told, hardly touched her. Her dad almost cried the few times he'd had to spank her on the tush for hitting her baby brother or that one time leaving his side at the grocery store when he'd told her not to. He held her over his knees and slapped her bottom one time, and that was it. What really hurt Laura was him hugging her so tight afterward and whispering into her ear all crackly, "I thought I'd lost you forever." But that's not what the nurse had asked. So Laura couldn't have known how the rest would unfold. She thought the nurse's question was innocent, a question she asked every boy and girl who came in to see her. The school called the authorities, who removed her and her baby brother from the house, and it took weeks to sort through it all and get them back into their home, with their parents who loved them. Laura still cried when she talked about the hurt she'd caused her mom and dad. And how ugly people had been to her, those who said they were there to help. Every time she tried telling them she wanted to go home to be with her mommy and daddy, they insisted she was better off here. But they didn't hug her at night, they didn't read to her, they didn't tuck her in.

When Ms. García says the counselor's there to help, you think about your cousins, how many weeks the authorities had spent on "helping" her and her brother. You don't need that kind of help. What are they going to do, remove you from your house and place you, where? Who takes in teenagers? Nobody, that's who. You've been taking care of yourself for a long while now. You've done a pretty good job so far, you think.

"Sorry, Miss, but I'm not going to no nurse or counselor."

"But . . . " Ms. García is on the verge of tears again.

You see in her eyes that she means well. But she doesn't know what would happen later. All your plans to leave town would be trashed. You want to be on your own, be your own person, paint, but if you go to the nurse right now, you'll belong to the State. *They don't care about me,* you think. *I'll be just a case number to them. They won't listen to me, trust that I can take care of myself like I've been doing. Where were they years ago when they should've pulled me from my house and put me in with some other family with a mom and dad who didn't make you lock yourself in a bathroom? Where are they now, when my mom's getting pushed around and knocked in the face and stomach? She's the one who needs help. It's not a sitcom plot, problem resolved by show's end.* You think, *Add five minutes to any of those shows right at the end there, and the actors, the director, the writers, they won't know what to do with themselves. That's where I'm living right now, inside those extra five minutes with no counselor to help me.*

But you notice the hurt in Ms. García's eyes, so you say, "Okay, I'll go to the counselor's office. But on my own. I don't need you to hold my hand."

You aren't lying about going to see the counselor. Now you do want to, but not for this. You'll go to find out what you have to do to enroll in one school or another in San Antonio. You haven't filled out any applications yet, but why not start now? You'll have one diploma soon, why not a second?

You hug Ms. García and say, "Thanks. You don't know how much you've helped."

You smile at her and walk down the hall toward the counselor's office.

CHAPTER TEN

BETO—6:48 AM, March 27TH

After finishing his paper route, Beto's dad asked if he wanted to be dropped off at school. Beto said no, that if it was okay with him, could they make a day of it? "Sure, *m'ijo*, but you know you can't miss many more days of school or . . . "

"Yeah, but, as if school's not a drag enough, I wouldn't be able to concentrate after . . . after last night."

Beto, Sr. drove on in silence. It wasn't so dark out now, but he kept the headlights on. "*M'ijo,*" he said after a few miles had passed.

"Yes?" Beto looked at his dad who was keeping a careful eye on the road.

Beto had never known his dad not to pay careful attention to whatever he was working on, including his driving. He always kept watch for cars behind him, beside him, in front. Even when there weren't any in sight, he was watchful. "You can never be too careful," he'd said to his boys plenty of times. It was probably the one thing about his dad that bothered Beto the most, how uptight he was about everything—the man never took chances. Whatever it was had to be a sure thing before the old man acted on it. For example, he always calculated in his head how much a thing would cost with taxes thrown in and added at least a few dollars' buffer before he considered buying it. Then he'd have to know that the money was in hand and that spending whatever amount on this purchase wouldn't take from the real everyday expenses like food and clothes, bills, the rainy day when one of them had to go to the doctor.

Last time he bought something big was a lawnmower to replace the one almost as old as Roelito, as far as Beto could remember. It'd taken Beto, Sr. a year-and-a-half to decide to buy their new lawnmower. In the meantime, he'd drag out the old one from the shed and tear it apart and put it back together again, then push and pull, struggling the whole time to mow the lawn. "You're not Dr. Frankenstein, Dad. One of these days, no lightening bolt big enough will bring this bad boy back to life. It's time to get a new one, don't you think, Dad?" Roelito had joked once. Their dad had come in sweating, his T-shirt so drenched that they could see his curly chest hair through it. Beto laughed and said, "Yeah, Dad. This one's had it. Admit you're the Mexican you know you are and put this one up on blocks in the backyard next to the other old one."

Beto, Sr. also laughed but just barely. "Laugh at the old man now, boys, but you got to squeeze every bit of worth out of anything and everything. I've kept this one going off the parts from the last one. I'll retire this one soon." But he didn't. Not for another year-and-a-half.

Beto couldn't figure out his dad. It wasn't like they were hurting for cash. The house and both cars were paid for. It wasn't like the old man needed this paper route. Truth be told, Beto was kind of embarrassed about his dad's route. "Isn't that a job for the teenie-bops, Dad?" he asked him when he'd first taken the work.

"A job's a job, *m'ijo*," he'd answered. "Hard work never hurt a man."

But a paper route? Beto thought. He never told a single one of his buddies at school what his dad did as a second job. He hadn't even wanted to tell Jessy, thinking she'd laugh about it, laugh in his face, at him. But she didn't. She looked him in the eye and said, "That's something. Your dad's a trip. Must be saving up for something good." Beto had never thought about it like that. Just figured his dad was being Dad.

The day he went to the store to get the new lawnmower, Beto remembered, it was a big to-do. Beto, Sr. got dressed, then put on his cowboy hat and boots. He went to Sears by himself, and when he came home, he didn't put together the new mower yet. He left it in the box for another two weekends and used the old one again and again: "No sense putting miles on the new one when the old one still has a heartbeat." And when he did retire it, it ended up next to the old, old machine, and that one he didn't get rid of either. "For parts," he'd told his wife. "You never know. Better safe than sorry."

Today, on their way to his dad's second job, Beto thought his dad was being extra quiet around the subject of last night. So was he. Beto had gotten scared last night. One thing that scared him was that he had it in him to raise a hand to his own father. Another just as huge was that Roelito had seen them at each other's throats like dogs. And the last thing, this one really scared him whether he liked to admit it or not, was that his dad had lost all confidence in him, had been so angry that he wanted Beto out of the house, had said he was done with him.

So they had to talk about it. Enough with beating around the bush.

"Dad, about last night. I'm sorry."

It was weird listening to himself saying this to his dad. He'd said it a few times before when he was a kid whether he meant it or not, for big and little things. But right now, in the car, the window rolled down and the cool fresh air on his face, saying he was sorry, his chest hurt. He felt like he'd cry if he went on talking. So he shut up. Let some time pass. Let the cool morning wind blow on his face.

"So am I, *m'ijo*," said his dad.

Now Beto's chest hurt more. His dad had taken a big gulp of air there at the end, like he'd run out of it.

Again, they drove in silence. There was a ton of construction work going on along the expressway, had been for too many months now, and even though there was hardly any traffic on the road this early in the morning, and even though the work crews weren't out, Beto, Sr. slowed the car down to 45 mph when the blinking sign said to drive 50. "Take care," the sign flashed, "my daddy's working today."

"I wish you could see it my way, Dad. How I figure it, you've done a good job raising me. Really. I don't do any of the stuff you think I do. You put that in my head a long time ago: no drugs, no smoking, no drinking, treat women with respect, don't be afraid of a little hard work and sweat. I got it then, Dad. I got it to this day. I know how hard a worker you are, how you love us, how you love Mom. I've seen it day in day out with my own eyes. Just because I don't follow the rules the same way as you doesn't mean I'm not following them."

Beto, Sr. kept quiet. Like he wanted Beto to go on, like he was really trying to hear what Beto was saying.

"Dad, the best thing you could've done for me, ever, was to teach me to be myself." Beto put his hand out the window, letting it whip up and down in the air current. "I don't behave like I do at school because my friends are pushing me to do it. Nobody, I mean nobody, Dad . . . "

No matter how hard he tried to look at his dad, he couldn't, so he looked at his hand outside the window instead. "Nobody but me, myself, makes me do what I do. And it's not that I want to cause problems for you and Mom. I've grown up, Dad. Like it or not, I'm my own man." But why couldn't he look at his dad? "I'm the one responsible for myself, now, not you. You should respect that."

"I can respect that, *m'ijo*, but you need to respect that I'm still your father, and Roelito's. I can't let things go like they've been going recently, loosen up just because you say, 'Look at me, Dad, I'm a man already, treat me like one.' You're still my responsibility, living under my roof. I mean, you're still in school. I don't mean to sound like a jerk, but that's how it's got to be. Maybe I'm old-fashioned . . . You young kids today, I can't figure you guys out. You have it so much easier than we ever did growing up, and you're—I don't know what—but like you expect to be treated like adults before you are. Like you deserve it. You don't. Not automatically."

A huge flashing arrow let them know the right lane was coming to an end, so Beto, Sr. put his left blinker on and eased over. The man even looked over his shoulder to see if anyone could've snuck up on them.

Beto, Sr. continued, "Things can't keep going like they are, you know? Either you give or I do, and I've got one more boy in the house to worry about raising right without having to think about how things'll go wrong if Roelito sees me buckle under your pressure. I know you're a good boy. I want to believe you don't drink and smoke, but what am I supposed to think when you break even my small rules? If you're true in the little things, the Bible says, you'll be true in the big ones. The same goes for the opposite." Beto, Sr. looked in the rearview mirror. "You're older and more mature than Roelito is in so many ways. I know that, but if he sees me, right now, give an inch to you, later, maybe sooner than later, he'll be pushing for his own inch, more likely two or three inches. I can't have that."

His fingers were beginning to tingle, so Beto pulled his hand in and rubbed at it. "Yeah, but you know how Roelito is, completely different from me. The kid's book-smart, actually enjoys school, and has plans for college. He thinks way different than I do. He knows better."

"You're right and wrong, Beto. I remember how you used to be not too long ago. In middle school, you couldn't get enough homework. You read so much back then. Somewhere between then and now you changed. I'm not saying for the worse, I'm just saying maybe it was my fault."

Beto looked at his dad now. The sun was beginning to break the horizon now. In the pinkish light, Beto thought his dad's face looked soft. Like in that portrait Jessy did of him with charcoal pencils, the one she'd given to him. He'd put it in his science book to keep it flat and safe. Soft around the edges, like Jessy looked through the screen last night, that's what his dad's face looked like now.

"I always go over it in my head, *m'ijo*. About the time you started to act up in your classes, I was still drinking. And I can't help thinking that maybe if I had quit earlier than I did. . . . Or maybe I wasn't providing for you like your friends' dads were. Maybe I didn't talk to you enough. Or when I did, I said the wrong things."

"No, Dad, it wasn't that."

And right now, Beto honestly couldn't think of how he could blame his dad for the way Beto had changed back in those days. He'd just gotten tired of school one day. He'd never really cared for reading. He found out that book learning wasn't for him. And when his teachers noticed the change, slowly, almost too small to see, they started behaving differently toward him, no longer smiling when they called his name at the beginning of class, no more pats on the back during lunchtime. Instead, there was a new roughness to their voices when they said his name. But it was nothing his dad did. Just him. Could he tell this to his dad now? Or ever?

"I also know your baby brother looks up to you, a lot," Beto, Sr. said. "I've seen how lately he's been trying to be more and more like you, the way he's combing his hair, the way he's walking. Sure, he's got plans for college, studies all the time, but he's still got too many years to go before he gets started on that part of his life. A lot can change for him in that time."

Now Beto, Sr. took his eyes off the road and looked at Beto, who saw the look coming from the corner of his eye and snapped his head to look back at his dad.

"You want him to dump his dreams? And he will if he doesn't know I'm the backbone in the house. He's at that age, Beto. He needs me to be this way right now, more than you need to be left alone by me. You've got to know, *m'ijo*, that when I treat you the way I do, it's not just you I'm thinking about, it's also him. So Roelito can't think, even for a second, I'm not the one making the decisions for you guys. Maybe you are ready to be your own man, but I don't think Roelito is. I've got him to think about.

You'll be out on your own soon enough. And when you're gone he'll still be at home."

"I understand that, Dad, but still . . . "

Man, it was getting deep for Beto. Even though he'd thought of leaving home any day now, had run away last night even, he never once thought his own dad, probably his mom too, had also considered it. This was serious for him. His future would soon enough be in his own hands.

" . . . But . . . "

"No buts, *m'ijo*. Be the man you claim to be."

Beto, Sr. took one hand from the steering wheel and patted his son on the thigh, then squeezed it so tight that it hurt Beto.

Beto looked down at the brown hand, at the knuckles, at the fingers and thumb. He wanted to squeeze his own hand under his dad's and keep it warm there for as long as possible. But Beto, Sr. snatched the hand and its warmth back and wrapped its fingers around the steering wheel again. Where it had been on Beto's thigh was still warm and hurt some. He felt even now how it had squeezed him, how strong his father's fingers were.

"*M'ijo*, you got two months to go till your graduation. Stick it out at home like you've done at school. You've been a big old fly in their ointment, *m'ijo*. I laugh every time they think you're done, but you keep going back for more. You don't know how proud that makes me. Last time I talked to your counselor, he told me everybody's about given up on you, myself included, if I'm honest. But you haven't quit. And I don't care that we've counted on you quitting school like you've quit everything else. I'll tell you what, *m'ijo*, they don't know you, they don't know the same man that I know this morning. The one who just a few minutes ago admitted he was sorry. That takes guts. That's being a man. They look at you all wrong. They think because you don't want to play their silly sports or get high grades that that's who you're going to be later in life. I hear how you talk to your brother, telling him he can't follow in your footsteps and be a quitter, that he needs to do right by our family, that he needs to go to college, shoot for the stars. That's one thing you've never quit at: telling him that he needs to keep going. And last night, when you left, I was sad, but proud too because you walked away when it counted. Does that make sense?"

Beto shook his head.

"I'm the adult between us. I shouldn't have let it get that far. But I lost it. And instead of you acting like a punk, you acted like the man. You know what that tells me? That you were on the edge of quitting our family, but you didn't. You left, walked away from a fight when it really mattered. Because, yes, you are a man. I saw it in your eyes right there at the end, how you were thinking of Roelito seeing us being stupid and selfish. You put me to shame, *m'ijo*, because you were strong enough to know when to turn away from a fight." All that time, his voice was deep, serious, even. "All I'm saying is, we need to keep thinking of Roelito. He'll be watching us with eagle eyes from now on. And you don't know how hard it's going to be for me to tell him I messed up acting like an idiot last night and that I think you're the better man, but I'm going to tell him. Tonight, as soon as I'm home from work, I'm going to tell him like it is."

They were quiet again. Beto wanted to say all the same things to his dad, how he was the one in the wrong, how if he could go back in time and fix things for himself, for his mom and dad, for Roelito, he'd jump at the chance, how he didn't see last night's fight the same way his dad saw it, as though last night he walked away. He hadn't. He'd run away. Like Jessy said in her letter. He'd actually wanted to quit, felt all last night in the dumpster that he'd really and truly done that, quit his family. And that hurt most of all. He didn't know where to start telling his dad any of this, couldn't figure out what the first word should be. He thought that if he could find that first word there'd be no stopping him. But what was that word? So in place of words, he reached out a hand, grabbed his dad by the arm and squeezed it, held it tight there for a good long way.

"What do you say if when we get home tonight, *m'ijo*, at the dinner table, Roelito sees us together? Not like best friends, not like I'm the winner and you're the loser, or vice versa. But as men, with respect for each other. For the family. For him. He's got to see that from the both of us."

Beto thought that was nice how his dad just let him know he wanted his son home tonight, had just told him home was still home.

"Good plan, Dad." That's all Beto could muster.

Later in the day, on one of his topsoil dump runs, Beto, Sr. told Beto, "Listen, son. Your mom and I've been putting money away for the both of you. Your pile's a bit bigger than your brother's, as it should be. You're older, we've been saving for you longer. It's not much, around $3,000."

Beto's eyes widened.

"Oh, it only sounds like a lot, *m'ijo*. It goes fast when it's yours. Anyway, I wanted you to use it for school. But it's for whatever you want. Your mom and I were going to wait to give it to you on graduation. But I'll hand it over to you sooner if you want. We'll go to the bank at lunch today and I'll sign it over to you, no strings, all yours to spend it however you want. In two months you can start looking for your own place, get a job, really be on your own."

"Dad, I don't know what to say."

"Ah, *m'ijo*, if I could it'd be more."

"Dad, no. That's more than . . . it's something I wasn't even expecting. I just . . . "

Man, for a talker, Beto found himself without words today. His parents all this while had been putting money aside for him, thinking about him, about making his future a bit easier getting started. And all he could say was, "Man, Dad, thanks."

"Two months, *m'ijo*. What do you say?"

"Two months. You got my word."

They shook on it, then they were quiet the rest of the way to their next appointment. Someone was waiting for the load of topsoil that would even out a crooked lawn in order to grow something on it.

CHAPTER ELEVEN

JESSY—4:12 PM, March 27TH

You don't much care that someone else has taken your usual seat on the bus after school. You open up your notebook, flip through all the materials the counselor gave you, and it doesn't bother you either that maybe others might see what you're so taken by. You're checking out a more concrete future for you, right there in front of you, on your lap, in full color. You look at the pictures of a couple of different campuses available to you in San Antonio, and the counselor even sneaked in a few pamphlets from El Paso, and one for an art school in San Francisco. That's way out there.

When you first hopped on the bus, you saw Roel, but he was staring out the window at his own world. Even if he'd looked your way, you most likely would've just smiled at him, found your own place to sit.

Where you sit is interesting, right next to Chela, that skinny girl who lives across the street with long, long brown hair, ribbons in it that always match her shoes. *She's a pretty girl*, you think, and want to say so. You don't. She's all kinds of shy, always looking down at her feet. You two have never talked like maybe neighbors should. And she's never mentioned knowing you stood up for her that time. You guess not, because she still wears tons of makeup. *Whatever possesses a girl to wear so much makeup?* In weather like this, with hardly a bit of eye makeup yourself, you feel like you're melting away. Chela's worse, wiping away her face, dripping like a Dali. You like that—already thinking like an artist, seeing like one. You don't like the image of her like that, though. You try thinking about something else.

Beto comes into your mind. *Too bad for him if he can't figure out for himself where he needs to be. He quickly pops out of your head.* You think of your parents but not in a poor Mom-and-Dad kind of way. You won't miss them so much when you leave, even though your leaving will mean your Mom will be on her own. But you don't allow yourself to think any of that.

You think about yourself this afternoon. Too many people who should've been keeping you in mind, looking out for your best interests, haven't been doing it. It had to be a teacher to see how far you'd gone already. It was Ms. García who put her arms around you like a mom should and gave you a shoulder to cry on like a dad should. A teacher, for goodness' sake. Not her responsibility to do so. In the end, who else but you to think about yourself? You, that's who.

Nobody's expecting your next move. Your teachers and classmates will probably ask themselves, "Really? Jessy? College?" They'll have no clue when you started thinking about it. And they'll be part right. You've never given even the slightest impression that you thought about going to college. But that's not to mean you have not thought about it seriously.

Now the bus is lurching to a stop over at the corner where you always get off. It's hot out and bright. Chela gets off right after you do. She says hello and you say, "Hey, there." You look at her smiling at you, a thin scar down the side of her face from the temple to the jaw on her right side. *So that's what she's hiding with so much makeup.* She waves bye. You'll have to remember the scar and paint her one day.

On the short walk to your house, you decide you'll come clean to your mom about what's been going on with you, what your plans are. You pat your notebook, nod, and plod on.

CHAPTER TWELVE

ROELITO—4:16 PM, March 27TH

I don't even have to look around me on the bus. I know Beto's not on it. Not this afternoon. So I'm thinking he's gone. Gone gone. I don't know where to, and right now I don't care. The farther away the better. And the reality of it doesn't hit me until right now, as we're pulling out of the school campus onto the expressway: He won't be at the house when I get there. All this time I've been thinking it's all about him or me. I should've been thinking about my mom. About my dad. How they must be feeling.

Beto's so selfish. All this time he's been the one who makes Mom and Dad worry so much over him. Every call from school about him is trouble, and how many times has Mom fallen asleep crying over him? She's all patient with him, never screams at him, even defends him against Dad yelling about him sometimes, and they end up fighting each other, and Beto usually wins out. Mom and Dad end up not talking to each other for days, and they talk to me and Beto all forced-like.

And with last night, I can only imagine how much a wreck Mom's been all day, especially being all alone in the house. I should've called to check in on her. *Stupid! Why didn't I? No, I was looking for Beto all day, fighting with Howie, dreaming about how I'll rule the UIL math team next year, already making up acceptance speeches for all the awards I'll win.* In that way, I'm no better than Beto. I mean, all day today when it wasn't about Beto Beto Beto, it was all about me me me. But what about Mom? What about Dad? Whenever I started thinking about Beto, I pushed Dad out of my head. I had enough without having to deal with him yet. I can't even imagine what he's been going through this whole entire day at work.

I need to let him know as soon as he comes in from work tonight that I don't know any other dad who's looked out for his family like he has. Every time we've been in need, he's come through. For all of us, Beto included. Beto especially.

That one time a few weeks ago, a Saturday night at church youth group, Beto got into it with Miguel, one of the pastor's sons, arguing about this or that. They exchanged some blows, and Beto got the better of Miguel. Knowing Beto, the scuffle was over something stupid, like him still wanting to call the pastor's daughter on the phone after her curfew, no matter what the pastor had said about it. The pastor drove Beto home and asked to speak in private to my dad. So they went outside and talked calmly for a few minutes. Then Dad turned his back on the pastor and stomped into the house, saying, "Nobody, nobody will ever call one of my boys a loser."

Turning his back like he did was a big deal for Dad, especially on the church pastor. My dad had only in the last year or so started going to church and was happy about it. He'd taken on responsibilities, like a bus route on Sunday mornings, and cleaning up the church building twice a month, and going out on visitations. The pastor also asked him if he'd mind getting on the ballot as a deacon for the next vote. My dad got the vote, and now he was walking away from the pastor. For a couple of Sundays, Dad didn't look too happy in church. He fulfilled his responsibilities, but it was like going through the motions. Then one Sunday, he invited the pastor for lunch at a restaurant and, according to my mom, my dad humbled himself and apologized to the pastor for turning his back. He said his son's behavior was a poor reflection on his skills as a dad, that he'd have to work harder on that, and would the pastor keep him and his family in prayer? I really couldn't imagine my proud dad kowtowing to anybody. But he did, all because of Beto.

And to see him last night, in that place, having to fight off his son. Talk about a wreck. I have to tell him that no matter what happened between the two of them, it wasn't his fault; it was Beto being an idiot.

When I get home, I don't know how it'll be, but I know this much, both Mom and Dad are going to get the biggest, fattest hugs from me. I'll tell them they don't have to worry about me. I'll join UIL math, keep my nose in the books, then go off to college. They can count on me. I can see what'll happen: they'll both give me some tired smiles, hug me back, my mom especially hard. But they'll still be worried about their other son. The one straying-away sheep. Who can blame them, right?

Look at me. I'm only brothers with him and see how I've wasted all my time during this ride home, all of today as a matter of fact, worrying over him. If he's going to be the big man he says he is, then he needs to man up, start acting like it, take responsibility for himself, somehow, anyhow, keep mom and dad from worrying so much. Humble himself to Dad like Dad did for him with the pastor. I'll go out looking for him later, tell him I think he's turned into the biggest jerk in the world. I don't know what I've been thinking all along, wanting to follow in his footsteps, thinking he was the coolest guy ever, and taking his side when he and dad argued. But here recently he's been nothing but a punk to me, a big self-centered fat-head baby, fighting in church, making Mom cry all the time, and Dad worry.

CHAPTER THIRTEEN

BETO—4:32 PM, March 27TH

Beto, Sr. told his boss he was cutting out a little early, if that was okay with him: "Family business, you understand."

His boss told him it was okay, then said to Beto, "He's a good man, your dad. Can always count on him."

Beto nodded: "Yeah. Yeah he is."

So he and his dad got home earlier than usual, beat the school bus home. Beto's mom was at her sewing machine. She must've been really into it and must not have noticed them come home because she jumped from her place when Beto, Sr. said, "Amor."

She looked at them, and Beto noticed her face was puffy and her eyes were irritated from crying. He knew she was deep in worry because sewing was what she did when she needed to calm herself. Maybe the rhythm of the whirring motor, the up and down of the needle and thread. Something did it for her.

"I should have called you, Amor," Beto, Sr. said. "He's been with me all day."

"Yes, you should have," she said. She kept to her side of the room, over by the machine, next to the window, behind her the wall unit blowing cool air into the room. "So, what's this?" She pointed at the two of them.

"Mom," Beto said. "I jumped into the car this morning, before Dad left for work. And all day, we've been talking. Working some things out."

"So you see, Amor, I didn't have a chance to call. We talked and worked all day long, nonstop, not even for a proper lunch." He pointed to his lunchbox. "Most of it's still warm."

"Well," she said, "you'll have lunch for tomorrow then." She took a few steps toward them, then she reached out for her husband's arm, grabbed him by the elbow and pinched him on the loose skin there.

"Ow," he said.

"That's for not calling. And this," and here she reached up and kissed him, "this is for . . . ," and her voice broke up some. "Well," she said, gathering herself, "well, for this." She put a soft palm up to Beto's cheek and an arm around Beto, Sr.

CHAPTER FOURTEEN

JESSY—5:39 PM, March 27TH

You hear your mom come in. She plops down at the kitchen table. Thinking this is as good a time as any other, you take all the brochures and pamphlets and spread them in front of her.

"And this?" she says.

"Mom, we haven't really talked about this much, but after school, I mean right after graduation, I'm leaving, going to college. I don't know which one of all these, but somewhere."

Your mom sits quietly, staring at the brochures.

"So?" you say.

"What so?" she asks.

"What do you think, Mom?"

"What am I supposed to think?"

"I don't know. Something. *Some*thing."

"My daughter, out of the blue, today tells me she's got plans to leave home. Go off to college . . . " She rifles through the pamphlets in front of her. "Where to? Oh, look, San Francisco." She holds that brochure up to your face. "So, she's leaving, setting her sights half a country away. If that's what you've decided to do, that's that."

Your mom collects all the brochures, taps them together on the table, and hands the bundle back to you. You take it and turn.

"Jessy," she says.

You stop but don't look back. "Yes?"

"What do you want for supper?"

"Whatever. Fix anything you want. I'll be in my room."

CHAPTER FIFTEEN

ROELITO—4:48 PM, March 27TH

When I get home, it doesn't surprise me to see Dad's car parked in the driveway. Of course he's home. He was probably thinking about Mom all day and even left work to be with her. What does throw me off is that the closer I am to the front door, the more I smell dinner, and isn't it just a bit too early for that?

I walk in the house, and now I'm really puzzled. I see Dad and Beto sitting at the dinner table. Mom's moving around, setting the table, a little slouchy at the shoulders. My dad has his arms crossed and he's still in his work uniform, and there's Beto at his regular spot, opposite Dad, and he's got a quiet look on his face, his hand on his left thigh. They all look tired to me. I feel exhausted. And seeing them all after a long day at school, not knowing anything, I'm confused.

The last person I thought I'd see home is Beto. But there he is. Except for the quiet, everything seems normal, another dinner at the López house, as usual: soft and greasy corn tortillas wrapped around crumbled beef, lettuce, and tomato, cheese, and avocado slices. Beans, rice. Three tacos a piece to start. Like any other dinner, only earlier. And except for what happened last night hanging over all of us.

But there we are, sitting at the table. What are we supposed to be? One big happy family? Beto's so quiet and eating without looking up, and Dad's chewing on his taco and undoing the top button on his shirt. It's all so calm, but still it's scary.

It doesn't register with me. Then Beto looks up all of a sudden and says, "Dad. . . . "

The rest of us stop what we're doing. Dad had started on the second button, I was halfway raising my glass of grape juice to my mouth, and Mom was wiping at her mouth with the paper napkin. I look at Dad and not Beto. Mom does too. Dad's the only one looking at Beto.

"Dad," he says, "about what I did last night . . . Mom, Dad, Roelito . . . " At my name, I turn toward Beto. He's facing me. "I'm sorry to all of you. It was wrong what I did and said."

Mom sneaks a breath, Dad gets back to his button, but I can see his fingers fumbling with it, then he says, "Thank you, *m'ijo*. I'm sorry also."

Beto stands and walks around the table to where Dad is. "I'm sorry, Dad. You're my father, and I shouldn't have disrespected you like that," he says.

My mom's crying. I get back to my grape juice and tacos. I can't believe what's going on here. I look up to see Beto extend his hand to Dad.

"I should have done this last night. You were right, Roelito."

Dad and Beto shake hands, and Dad stands up and hugs Beto.

CHAPTER SIXTEEN

Getting Ready for Tomorrow, March 27th, Late PM

That night, everybody's in bed well before midnight.

The lights out in their room, Beto feels like talking: "Hey, bro. You awake?"

Roe doesn't answer, although he's awake.

"Bro," Beto calls again, this time a bit louder, but Roe doesn't stir. Roe faces the window, his eyes shut, breathing heavy and steady like he knows will fool anyone. Then he hears Beto real close: "Roe . . . " Roe feels his mattress shift under Beto's weight.

"It's cool, bro," Beto says. "You don't have to be awake for this if you don't want. I just have to get some stuff off my chest, right? Last night, well, I'm such a punk, man. I feel bad enough what I did to Dad. He's never been anything but a good dad, I know that. I mean, he gets on my nerves, pushy, feels like he's stunting my growth sometimes, you know, but he's still my dad, I'm still his son. I shouldn't have fought with him. Period.

"But what I did worse than anything last night—letting you see any of it. I swear, bro, if I could take us back in time, the way it would've happened was this way: Dad would've busted me outside the room like he did, we'd gone outside to talk it out, he would've screamed at me, and I would've just taken it like before. That way you wouldn't have woken up, and if you had, all you would've seen was me standing there taking what Dad was dishing out. You would've seen me act like a real son. Like a man.

"I hope you're just faking sleep, bro. That you heard all this. I'll ask you in the morning whether you did or not. If you didn't, I'll tell it all to you again. It's important you know I didn't do right by you, bro. It's important you know I'm just a fool, not so good as an older brother. Not so good as a son. But I'll try better now. *Pues*, good night, bro."

He gets up off the bed and hears a sob, more like a gulp for breath, but he doesn't turn back, makes like he doesn't hear it, just hops onto his bed, and that's that for them.

Roe is crying but he doesn't want to let on that he is, so he shoves his face into his pillow. He thinks he should've faced his brother and let it all out, about how all of today he'd been angry with him, had even hated his guts and wished he'd never come back, and that, yes, he'd been a punk to Dad because a real man doesn't hit his own father no matter what, and doesn't make his mom cry all the time, that if Beto thought his little speech at dinner and this one right now could erase the fight, no way, it wouldn't. Sure he could forgive Beto, but forget what he'd done? Not hardly. It would be a long row to hoe. He'd have to start at the beginning, at square one. Prove himself to be the cool guy Roe had thought he was before. And he didn't know if Beto had it in him to follow through. That's what he would've said if he had not been crying with his face in his pillow, faking sleep. And Roe thinks, *I don't know if I can tell him all of that in the morning. That's a long way away, and what if I forget it, or he changes his mind and doesn't ask me if I heard what he said to me right now?* So Roe turns onto his back, then raises himself up on an elbow: "Beto," and he tells him everything, the both of them crying.

In bed, Jessy feels like crying. She won't, though. She's cried enough. Didn't she make enough of a fool of herself at school today in front of Ms. García? She'd cried then because it had been too heavy a weight to carry herself, to have stuck it out at home all this time, and for two more months still, home like it was, all ugly and violent. And when she talked to her mom about her plans to leave after graduation, all her mom said was, "You're gonna do what you're gonna do. You've always been stubborn like that," and after, hadn't Jessy taken all her college materials and hid herself in her bathroom and cried? Later, her mom knocked on her bathroom door and said, "Jessy, baby, dinner's almost ready. Your dad will be home soon." She didn't hear Jessy crying, or if she did, she didn't let on, and instead said, "Your Dad's not gonna like your news, not one bit, so let's just keep this a secret between the two of us. Let's wait on telling him, okay, baby?"

Jessy would've preferred it if her mom had said, "I don't want you to go, baby. That is, not without me. I'm sick and tired of him, too. Let's pack up and go now, just the two of us. You can study art like you've always wanted, and I'll get a job somewhere, and we'll make a go of it." And she would've answered, "I'm ready, Mom, let's go." But her mom didn't come through like that. She didn't want to make trouble with her dad. Jessy stayed in her bathroom and cried some more.

Jessy told herself, "Get it together, Jess. And no more of this boo-hooing and locking myself in." She wiped her face dry, walked out of the bathroom, and looked at all the brochures again, especially the San Francisco one. *Why not?*

Tomorrow morning, she'd find a computer in the library and email the school for an application packet. She read up on the San Francisco art scene, get all caught up.

So tonight, before going to bed, she opened the door to her room wide and left the bathroom door and her window open, then climbed into bed, no books, no music.

She takes her blanket and covers herself. She smiles and closes her eyes. She has so many ideas for paintings, all of them whizzing around her brain. *Tomorrow morning. Tomorrow, I'll get this ball rolling. No more locking myself in, no more running away. I've got a plan for myself.*

It had been a long day of crying for everyone, it seems. They'd all gone a good long way to get to sleep tonight. A bit worse for wear, but better on the whole, all of them. The day was over now. And tomorrow morning would bring a new day and with it, all new ups and downs. But tonight, it was a restful sleep.

Additional Piñata Books for Young Adults

Fitting In
Anilú Bernardo
2005, 208 pages, Trade Paperback
ISBN: 978-1-55885-437-6
$9.95, Ages 11 and up
Accelerated Reader Quiz #35022
Winner, 1997 Paterson Prize for Books for Young People and the 1997 Skipping Stones Honor Award

Trino's Choice
Diane Gonzales Bertrand
1999, 128 pages, Trade Paperback
ISBN: 978-1-55885-268-6
$9.95, Ages 11 and up
Accelerated Reader Quiz #35007
Named to the 2001-2002 Texas Lone Star Reading List; "Best Book of the Year," Young Adult category, ForeWord Magazine; and Recipient, Austin Writers' League Teddy Award for Best Children's Book

Trino's Time
Diane Gonzales Bertrand
2001, 176 pages, Trade Paperback
ISBN: 978-1-55885-317-1
$9.95, Ages 11 and up
Accelerated Reader Quiz #54653
Named to The New York Public Library's Books for the Teen Age 2002

Desert Passage
P. S. Carrillo
2008, 192 pages, Trade Paperback
ISBN: 978-1-55885-517-5
$10.95, Ages 11 and up
Accelerated Reader Quiz #127758

Riding Low on the Streets of Gold
Latino Literature for Young Adults
Edited by Judith Ortiz Cofer
2003, 192 pages, Trade Paperback
ISBN: 978-1-55885-380-5
$14.95, Ages 11 and up

Windows into My World
Latino Youth Write Their Lives
Edited by Sarah Cortez
Introduction by Virgil Suárez
2007, 272 pages, Trade Paperback
ISBN: 978-1-55885-482-6
$14.95, Ages 16 and up
Recipient, 2008 Skipping Stones Honor Award

Chicken Foot Farm
Anne Estevis
2008, 160 pages, Trade Paperback
ISBN: 978-1-55885-505-2
$10.95, Ages 11 and up
Accelerated Reader Quiz #123847
Finalist, Texas Institute of Letters 2008 Literary Awards

Creepy Creatures and Other Cucuys
Xavier Garza
2004, 144 pages, Trade Paperback
ISBN: 978-1-55885-410-9
$9.95, Ages 11 and up

A So-Called Vacation
Genaro González
2009, 192 pages, Trade Paperback
ISBN-13: 978-1-55885-545-8
$10.95, Ages 14 and up

The Throwaway Piece
Jo Ann Yolanda Hernández
2006, 192 pages, Trade Paperback
ISBN: 978-1-55885-353-9
$9.95, Ages 11 and up
Accelerated Reader Quiz #108531
Winner, 2007 Paterson Prize for Books for Young People, Finalist; ForeWord Magazine's Best Book of the Year 2006; Named to The New York Public Library's Books for the Teen Age 2007; and Winner, University of California, Irvine's Chicano / Latino Literary Prize

Additional Piñata Books for Young Adults

The Truth about Las Mariposas
Ofelia Dumas Lachtman
2007, 144 pages, Trade Paperback
ISBN: 978-1-55885-494-9
$9.95, Ages 11 and up

Versos sencillos / Simple Verses
José Martí
English translation by Manuel A. Tellechea
1997, 128 pages, Trade Paperback
ISBN: 978-1-55885-204-4
$12.95, Ages 11 and up

Named to the 1999–2000 Houston Area Independent School Library Network Recommended Reading List

My Own True Name: New and Selected Poems for Young Adults, 1984–1999
Pat Mora
Drawings by Anthony Accardo
2000, 96 pages, Trade Paperback
ISBN: 978-1-55885-292-1
$11.95, Ages 11 and up
Accelerated Reader Quiz #47265

Teen Angel
A Roosevelt High School Series Book
Gloria Velásquez
2003, 160 pages, Trade Paperback
ISBN: 978-1-55885-391-1
$9.95, Ages 11 and up
Accelerated Reader Quiz #85593

Tyrone's Betrayal
A Roosevelt High School Series Book
Gloria Velásquez
2006, 144 pages, Trade Paperback
ISBN: 978-1-55885-465-9
$9.95, Ages 11 and up
Accelerated Reader Quiz #110766

The Almost Murder and Other Stories
Theresa Saldana
2008, 144 pages, Trade Paperback
ISBN: 978-1-55885-507-6
$10.95, Ages 11 and up

Alamo Wars
Ray Villareal
2008, 192 pages, Trade Paperback
ISBN: 978-1-55885-513-7
$10.95, Ages 11 and up
Accelerated Reader Quiz #123846

My Father, the Angel of Death
Ray Villareal
2006, 192 pages, Trade Paperback
ISBN: 978-1-55885-466-6
$9.95, Ages 11 and up
Accelerated Reader Quiz #110738

Named to The New York Public Library's Books for the Teen Age 2007, *and Nominated, 2008-2009 Texas Library Association's Lone Star Reading List*

Who's Buried in the Garden?
Ray Villareal
2009, 160 pages, Trade Paperback
ISBN: 978-1-55885-546-5
$10.95, Ages 11 and up

Walking Stars
Victor Villaseñor
2003, 208 pages, Trade Paperback
ISBN: 978-1-55885-394-2
$10.95, Ages 11 and up
Accelerated Reader Quiz #35002